p. 1.

BUCKINGHAM HALL.

"Uncle Tom's Cabin"

CONTRASTED WITH

BUCKINGHAM HALL,

THE

PLANTER'S HOME,

OR,

A Fair View of both sides of the Slavery Question.

BY

ROBERT CRISWELL, Esq.

AUTHOR OF "LETTERS FROM THE SOUTH AND WEST."

"The master of a well ordered home, knoweth to be kind to his servants; yet he exacteth reverence, and each one feareth at his post."—*Tupper.*

NEW-YORK:

PRINTED AND PUBLISHED BY D. FANSHAW,

No. 108 Nassau-street.

....

1852.

TO

THE MEMORY OF

HENRY CLAY,

Whose lamented death, (shrouding the Nation in mourning, and filling the hearts of his countrymen with *sorrow* and *regret*,) occurring while these pages were in the hands of the publisher; this Book is dedicated, with *heartfelt sorrow*, as a small token of admiration of his great services in behalf of his country, and more especially of the last great act in the drama of his life, (to which it is supposed he fell a martyr,) viz: his noble efforts in endeavoring to allay the great agitation on the Slavery question, between the North and the South.

As every thing relating to that great man,

"Whose like we ne'er shall see again,"

Is deeply interesting, I will here introduce an incident which took place about the time he offered his celebrated compromise resolutions to the Senate.

A word of explanation in regard to the subject will be necessary:

A few years ago I visited the tomb of Washington, at Mount Vernon, and while searching for relics in the old vault, (his remains having been removed from it in 1837, to a new vault near by,) I fortunately found a fragment of his coffin with parts of the pall attached to it by two brass nails, which fragment I presented to Mr. Clay.

The same morning, whilst speaking before the Senate, he alluded to the subject as follows:

"I cannot omit, before I conclude, relating an incident, a *thrilling incident* which occurred prior to my leaving my lodgings this morning.

"A gentleman came to my room—the same at whose instance, a few days ago, I presented a memorial calling upon Congress for the purchase of Mount Vernon for the use of the public—and, without being at all aware of what purpose I entertained in the discharge of my public duty to-day, he said to me, 'Mr. Clay, I heard you make a remark the other day which induces me to suppose that a precious relic in my possession would be acceptable to you. He then drew from his pocket and presented to me the object which I now hold in my hand. And what, Mr. President, do you suppose it is? It is a fragment of *the coffin of Washington*—a fragment of that coffin in which now repose in silence, in sleep and speechless, all the earthly remains of the venerated Father of his country. Was it portentious that it should have been thus presented to me? Was it a sad presage of what might happen to that fabric which Washington's virtue, patriotism and valor established? No, sir, no. It was *a warning voice, coming from the grave* to the Congress now in Session, to beware, to pause, to reflect before they lend themselves to any purposes which shall destroy that Union which was cemented by his exertions and example. Sir, I hope an impression may be made on your mind, such as that which was made on mine, by the reception of this *precious relic.*"

This incident illustrates Mr. Clay's tact and ingenuity in seizing and turning to good account this and like circumstances. Little did I think when presenting that fragment, that two or three hours after, it would be, in the hands of Henry Clay, the means of producing more deep feeling and sensation in the Senate than had been witnessed for years. The Senators ceased talking and writing, and gave their whole attention to the Speaker, while profound silence reigned throughout the crowded galleries. Many were moved to tears.

What a subject this would have been for an artist! The venerable and immortal Clay, his commanding form stretched to its full height, and his eagle eye beaming with patriotism, holding in his right hand a part of *the coffin of Washington*, and conjuring his brother Senators, in the name of that great and good man, to spare that Union which was cemented by his exertions and example.

Though Mr. Clay was much engaged at the time I presented him with the relic, the next day I received the following note from him, which has not been given to the public before:

"H. Clay, with his respects, presents to Mr. Criswell many thanks for the *fragment* from the *coffin of Washington*, which he did him the favor to present to him. It is a *precious relic*, which Mr. Clay will *carefully preserve.*

"Wishing Mr. Criswell health and happiness, I am truly his friend, and obedient servant,

"H. Clay."

Washington, Jan. 30, 1850.

As an evidence of the estimate Mr. Clay put upon this relic, he, in his will, left a ring containing a part of it, to one of his dearest friends.

The Author.

PREFATORIAL.

The Author in laying this work before the public has but one motive in view, which is to contribute his mite *in endeavoring to allay the great agitation on the Slavery Question between the North and South, which threatens to dissolve our glorious Union; and as that talented authoress, Mrs. Stowe, in "Uncle Tom's Cabin," has increased that agitation, the author hopes to modify it somewhat, by representing the Planter and Slave in a more favorable light.*

Though living in the North, he has travelled extensively through the South, (having visited nine of the Southern States,) he therefore flatters himself that he gives a fair and impartial statement of both sides of the question.

Many of the incidents and stories related in the book came under his own observation, while others were given him by acquaintances.

If his motive is realized in the least degree, if the book proves to be one drop *of* oil *cast upon the* tempestuous sea *of* agitation, *his wishes will be accomplished.*

THE AUTHOR.

UNCLE TOM'S CABIN

CONTRASTED WITH

BUCKINGHAM HALL.

CHAPTER I.

" There is a Divinity that shapes our ends,
" Rough hew them as we will."

Colonel George Buckingham was a wealthy planter, whose residence was near Charleston, South Carolina. His whole establishment exhibited a style and magnificence uncommon in that place. Being descended from some portion of the English nobility, the Colonel made it a point to adopt their manners and customs in his own domain. Therefore, Buckingham Hall, which was situated in the centre of a fine park, adorned with stately forest trees and various kinds of ornamental shrubbery, was a splendid building of the Columbian Order, furnished with almost Oriental magnificence. He never went abroad without four horses to his carriage, and his household servants—all slaves—were, without exception, dressed in livery.

The Colonel was justly proud of his beautiful villa, from the cupola of which he could enjoy a delightful view of the fine harbor of Charleston, with Fort

Moultrie and Castle Pinckney in the distance. In this observatory was fitted up his library, with telescopes and other astronomical instruments, for though not a learned man, in the strict sense of the word, he was fond of literature and science, and employed a good part of his time reading and studying.

Although a man of sterling worth and good qualities, Colonel Buckingham had his weak points, especially in regard to his ancestral blood, which, he often boasted, had *not* "Crept through scoundrels ever since the flood," but was pure and aristocratic in its descent. From the researches he had made in the English books of Peerage, he had discovered that his grandfather's grandfather was a brother of one of the Dukes of Buckingham, therefore, he flattered himself that a few drops of noble blood were coursing through his veins; and on this was based the haughtiness and unbending pride of his character. However, to his slaves, he was uniformly kind and humane, and in return they loved him with all the native simplicity of their hearts. Colonel Buckingham had several plantations in Georgia and Alabama, on which were four or five hundred slaves, which he was in the habit of visiting at different periods of the year. All of them, and especially those near his person, were so attached to him, that if offered their freedom they would not accept of it if it would separate them from their master. They would have said that their condition was far better than that of the free negroes around them, that they had all the necessaries of life, and that when illness confined them at home, a physician was never wanting to attend them. Such indeed, is generally the feeling between the slave and a kind master: but alas! there are too many slave-holders whose cruelty makes them hated and feared by the unfortunate objects of their tyranny.

Colonel Buckingham was a widower, and had two children, a son and daughter. The son, Eugene, was, at the period of his introduction to the writer, about twenty-five years of age, tall, well-proportioned and rather good-looking. In disposition he was open-hearted, frank and generous to a fault; but it must be confessed that he possessed a pretty large share of vanity, which could be seen lurking in every lineament of his countenance. Like his father, he was inclined to boasting on subjects concerning himself; and would occasionally tell of his being at a brilliant party at the Charleston Hotel, given in honor of some foreign literary character; when he was told by a gentleman, that the ladies considered him a perfect resemblance of a certain Capt. S. the handsomest man in the room. There was also a degree of haughtiness in his manners which was far from pleasing; but when he desired to please, he could be as polite and affable as any. Yet, he would never humble himself in the least degree to obtain a favor of any man, there was too much pride and independence in his character for that. On the whole, however, he was much liked by his acquaintance, and his company considered quite an acquisition.

His sister Cora was a tall, graceful girl of nineteen, her hair and eyes were blackness itself; and in the latter was an expression of dreaminess and langour that was very fascinating. She had just returned from school, and was already quite a belle, for though not beautiful, there was a lady-like softness of manner, and a sweet insinuating smile, that were to the enthusiastic Southerners, irresistable. Still, accomplished as she was, her acquirements were merely superficial; she was weak-minded and indolent in character and disposition.

Eugene Buckingham had attended college in Columbia for several years, his father being determined he should be well educated; and in this he was not disappointed, for the young man graduated with honors. Well satisfied on this point, the Colonel began to think of a wife for the son-and-heir of his possessions. On looking around him, his choice fell upon the daughter of his nearest neighbor, Frederick Jones, Esq. whose plantation joined that of the Colonel, and which was well stocked with valuable slaves. Without consulting the wishes of Eugene, his father proposed the match to Mr. Jones, who received it with great favor, and immediately recommended it to his daughter Susanna, whose pleasure at the idea was extreme. It was all she wished—all she had striven to gain for the last year. She was a large, showy girl, with rather a pretty face, but her manners were *brusque* and masculine. She was fond of gayety, and was scarcely ever at home; and being a fearless rider, she raced and hunted as well as any of the young men.

She often visited at Buckingham Hall, although no favorite of Cora's; and as for Eugene, he kept as much as possible out of her way.

But being informed by his father of the alliance he had formed for him, the anger of the young man was uncontrollable; he did not, indeed, disguise his antipathy and disgust of the proposal, whereat his father was so exasperated that he threatened to disinherit him if he did not obey his commands. But Eugene left his presence without any reply.

Now, Mr. Jones had no education himself; and consequently considered that his children could do without it as well as he. Therefore he would not send his daughter to school, nor his son to college; for, said he, "I would be a fool to spend five or six hundred a year on their learning, when I can leave them a slave worth that amount for every year they would be there." So, as you may suppose, his sons and daughter grew up about as ignorant as their father.

Colonel Buckingham urged his son so often and so strenuously to pay his devoirs to Miss Jones, and her father so incessantly attempted to joke with him on the subject, that he became utterly disgusted at the idea of marriage; and inwardly vowed that he would never tie himself to any woman. Neither parents seemed to understand that Susanna was not the woman formed to excite the tender passion in a man of taste and feeling. Love is a delicate plant, that grows spontaneously in its native soil; it cannot be forced by artificial means; and if ever transplanted, it requires skillful and tender cultivation, else it withers and dies.

Although the Colonel wished the match on account of the young lady's possessions, Eugene was too noble minded to marry for wealth alone; nothing short of mental beauty and a gifted mind could interest a soul like his.

But at last, wearied out with the persecutions of the two fathers, and the irksome presence of the daughter, who was every day at Buckingham Hall, Eugene resolved to quit his home, and pay a visit to the North, disregarding the repeated threat of his father to disinherit him. Notwithstanding the respect he bore the author of his being, and the love he had for his sister, nothing could induce him to remain where life was to him a torment. Therefore, he suddenly took his departure from Charleston, much to the astonishment and chagrin of Frederick Jones, Esq. and his "very interesting" daughter Susanna, who, however, took the disappointment to heart much less than her father, for *he* had set his mind on annexing the plantations.

CHAPTER II.

"Upon thy heart there is laid a spell,
"Holy and precious—oh, guard it well!"—*Hemans.*

Although Eugene Buckingham, when in a fit of spleen, had vowed he would never marry, he had for more than a year been in love—not with any woman he had ever seen—but with an ideal that lay cradled in his heart. The fact was, a lady of New-York had been contributing for some time to the various periodicals and magazines throughout the States, under the *nom de plume* of Corinne Sunshine, and Eugene was so facinated by her writings, that he, enthusiastic fellow! fell in love with an imaginary being, a creature of perfection, which perhaps if ever found would prove nothing more than a mere mortal, likely enough, either old or ugly. But, although this thought sometimes passed through his brain, he immediately banished it, for the romance was so delightful that he would not suffer it to be dispelled. From the character of the lady's writings, he concluded *her* character and disposition to be as bright and sunshiny as her name, therefore she would be just the woman to please him. It was partly to discover the name and residence of his "soul's idol," that his intended destination was New-York, and it was with a heart full of hope and pleasing anticipations, that he boarded the splendid steamer Crescent City, bound for that port. After a speedy and agreeable voyage he arrived at the "Commercial emporium of the Union," and was soon established at the Astor House. Having with him a letter of introduction from a gentleman of Charleston to Capt. Coleman, that "Prince of Hosts," he received him like an old friend, and their acquaintance soon became a mutual pleasure.

Eugene spent a fortnight perambulating the city, and visiting the many places of amusement; and then thinking that he might discover his *inamorata* by seeking N. P. Willis, who is said to know nearly all the literary characters in Christendom; he called upon him, and on our hero's propounding the question, this gentleman promptly told him that the lady who wrote under the signature of Corinne Sunshine, was a Miss Julia Tennyson, daughter of Dr. Tennyson of La Fayette Place; but unfortunately for Eugene, Willis was not personally acquainted with her; so that to gain an introduction was yet an impossibility. But "as hope springs eternal in the human breast," the young man, on his way back to the hotel, endeavored to contrive some mode of obtaining a sight of the lady, that he might know at a glance whether his ideal was embodied in her. At last a thought struck him, and the next day he acted upon it. It was this: he bought at Stewart's an elegantly embroidered pocket handkerchief, and immediately proceeding to La Fayette Place, mounted the steps and rung the bell of No. —. The door was opened, and he inquired of the servant if Miss Tennyson was at home. Replying in the affirmative, she ushered him into an elegant parlor, and on asking his name, he replied that he was a stranger. The girl looked curiously at him for a moment, and then disappeared. Imagine his feelings —in the very house of his ideal—momentarily expecting her appearance, discomposed and agitated; but he felt he must be calm, or how was he to carry out his little piece of deception?

The long wished for moment arrived. Miss Tennyson stood before him—a creature of such exquisite loveliness that his eyes were dazzled, and for a moment his tongue was paralized. He could only bow, which she returned with stately grace, and asked, in a voice sweeter and softer than ever before dwelt upon his ear, what was the object of his visit.

Finding at last his utterance, he said, "Pardon my intrusion, but I found this hankerchief with your name upon it in an omnibus, and I could do no less than return it to you."

The young lady took the article in her hand and replied, "It is indeed my name, but sir, the handkerchief is not mine, it must belong to some other person; it is strange."

"So it is," echoed Eugene, (slightly blushing as his conscience reproved him for his deception,) "I was not aware there could be another lady of the name of her of whom I have heard so much."

"Perhaps," said Julia, smiling, "it was the other lady of whom you have heard."

Eugene shook his head—"No! But since it is not yours, excuse my intrusion."

"Not at all," replied Julia, politely, as the young man bowed himself into the street; and when the door closed he thought darkness had fallen upon the earth, for the vision that enlightened his soul for a few moments was no longer visible.

Our hero had now gained one object; he had seen his ideal, and found her to surpass his wildest dreams. She was apparently about nineteen, above the medium height, possessed a slender and graceful form, a sweet, soul-breathing countenance, large, liquid brown eyes, and hair of a glossy chestnut, that fell in a profusion of curls around her face and finely formed neck. Her beauty was of that rare kind formed to last for ever; if not in the world, in the hearts of those that bore its impress. It was so with Eugene; for weeks after, wherever he went, that vision of loveliness was before him; it was the theme of his meditations by night and by day.

One afternoon in the second week of June, our hero paid a visit to the Academy of Design, that place "where lovers oft do congregate," and while there, was surprised and delighted to meet Miss Tennyson, who was accompanied by an elderly lady. She did not appear to observe him as he stood at a distance, drinking in her beauty with all his soul. Then, as she moved on, he followed, still at a distance; for the time, entirely regardless of the magnificent paintings around him, as his whole mind was absorbed in the living picture. At length she stopped at a design that seemed to please her extremely, and Eugene gradually drew nearer. The painting was called the "Declaration:" it represented a young man standing by the side of a lovely girl and holding her hand; with love, tenderness, and anxiety depicted in his countenance, while she, with downcast eyes, and timid heart-revealing look, showed that his wishes would meet no refusal.

"Ah!" sighed Eugene to himself, "would that I and the lovely Julia were in the same situation, and that I were as sure of success as that young man."

Miss Tennyson at length exclaimed, as if unconsciously, "Beautiful! beautiful!"

"Beautiful, indeed!" echoed young Buckingham.

The young lady started and turned around. As her eyes fell upon him she seemed embarrassed, but made no sign of recognition.

"Excuse me, Miss Tennyson, I did not mean to intrude." She made no reply, but bowed and passed on. Eugene remained where he was, and shortly after, saw by a side glance that she was leaving the room. Having now nothing to interest him, he soon retraced his steps to his hotel. On the way he soliloquized as follows:

"Here I have been for a month without making her acquaintance; and how that acquaintance is to be made I do not imagine. She treats me so coolly too—I wish I could obtain an introduction—unfortunately I know no one that is acquainted with her. I regret that I left my home in the 'sunny South' on this Quixotic expedition—I almost despair—but no! I will not! 'Perseverance' is my motto, and I believe in the old adage, that 'the darkest hour is just before day,' therefore I will try again."

As he entered the Astor he met his friend Capt. Coleman, who addressed him with, "Ah, my young friend, so you have been walking out; I have got something for you." And he handed him a beautifully embossed note, which Eugene took and read as follows:

"Mr. Buckingham's company will be agreeable this evening at No. —, La Fayette Place."

The astonishment and delight of our hero cannot be expressed. He stood and stared at his friend without a word.

"Ha! ha!" laughed the Captain, "what is the matter?"

"Is this a hoax?'

"A hoax? no; what put that in your head?"

"I am not acquainted with anybody in that quarter."

"What of that, if they wish to be acquainted with you. The fact is, my dear Buckingham, I have said so much about the 'young Southerner' to Dr. Tennyson and his beautiful daughter, that they have a great desire to see you. There is no necessity of looking so scared; all you will have to do is to prepare yourself for the party and accompany me. Will you go?"

"Certainly," replied Eugene. And then, forgetting himself, he said aloud, "she will be surprised."

"Why?" exclaimed the other, "has she ever seen you?"

The young man blushed deeply, as he stammered out, "Yes—I—that is—she—I have seen her—I—"

"Ah, ha! I see, I understand. Well, we start at nine." And the amiable gentleman passed into the street laughing quietly to himself.

After tea Buckingham visited Cristadora's shaving saloon, under the Astor, and after a short space came forth greatly improved in the upper story. He then repaired to his chamber, and while dressing his thoughts were these:

"Day is at length beginning to dawn upon me; the clouds that have been hanging over me for weeks are now dispersing, leaving a clear opening in the bright blue sky of my existence. I feel that my presentiment will yet be crowned with success:

> 'It must be so,
> 'Else, why this longing hope, this fond desire?'

"I have always been a firm believer in predestination, for, if the 'hairs of our heads are all numbered, and not a sparrow falleth to the ground without His notice,' have we not reason to believe that an event of so much importance as marriage is arranged by Infinite Goodness? If so, might I not as well ascertain from the lovely Julia, to night, whether or not our lot is to be united? But, no; I will not be so abrupt: for if Providence ordains the ends, it also ordains the means by which those ends are accomplished."

Having finished dressing he took a last look in the mirror, and was quite satisfied with what he saw there,—for the reader will recollect that one of his failings was excessive vanity—and then descended to the ladies' parlor, where he remained making observations on the company, until summoned to the carriage by Captain Coleman.

CHAPTER III.

"The brightness of her cheek would shame the stars,
"As daylight doth a lamp; her eyes in heaven
"Would, through the airy region, stream so bright
"That birds would sing and think it were not night."

Eugene Buckingham and his companion said little on their way to the mansion of Dr. Tennyson, for our hero was too absent to converse, and the other had no inclination to interrupt his reverie. At length the carriage stopped before the door and the friends entered the house.

The large, brilliantly lighted parlors were filled with a goodly representation of the "*upper tendom*," and as they advanced, Eugene's visual organs scanned the rooms for the star and belle of the evening. He soon discovered her seated on an ottoman surrounded by a circle of gentlemen; and it was not surprising that a pang of jealousy shot with an electric thrill through his heart, "Should she happen to be engaged!" he thought.

"Come," said Coleman, with a meaning smile, "now for the introduction!"

Buckingham's heart leaped at the words, and he actually felt a trembling sensation creep over him, as, taking the arm of his friend, he approached with him the unconscious object of his adoration.

"Good evening, Miss Tennyson; allow me to present my friend Mr. Buckingham."

Julia raised her lustrous eyes, and an expression of strong surprise flitted across her countenance; and bowing with some embarrassment, she said, "I am happy to see you, sir."

Eugene bowed as politely as he knew how, and ventured to ask the honor of her hand for the dance, if not engaged.

She replied, "I am engaged for this set, but for the next I shall be happy."

Some of the young exquisites around her let fall their under lips with chagrin, and one or two, acquainted with the Captain, followed him to inquire "who the deuce that proud looking fellow was?"

On being informed that he was the only son and heir of a rich Southern planter, they begged for a presentation, and endeavored throughout the evening to make themselves as agreeable as possible to young Buckingham.

It was soon whispered about the room, who our hero was, and he became a *lion* at once. The young ladies bestowed on him their most fascinating smiles, but in vain; he, like Achilles, was invulnerable, save in one spot, and that, none had discovered but the gentle Julia.

As Eugene led Miss Tennyson to the dance, he felt, in his pride, full six inches taller, for was she not the most splendid girl in the room, and the "cynosure of all eyes?" She was simply dressed, in rich white embroidered muslin, without a single ornament save a blush rose in her dark hair, yet overshadowed every lady present, as in the dance

> "She moved a goddess, and she looked a queen."

All indeed acknowledged her superior charms except some over-dressed maiden ladies, whose eyes were blinded by pure envy alone. Our hero himself was in raptures with her beauty and grace, and charmed with the brilliance of her conversation.

But, "all that's bright must fade," and so thought Eugene, as

> "The silent hours stole on,
> "And flaky darkness broke within the East,"

compelling him, with the other guests, to depart. As he wished Julia good morning he begged permission to call on her, which she granted without hesitation.

Dr. Tennyson was a Scotchman, and a gentleman of the old school, proud, learned, and talented, with many good qualities both in mind and heart. Though not possessed of a fortune, he had an excellent practice, and always lived fully up to his income, so that whoever proposed for the hand of his daughter must take her portionless. This Eugene was fully aware of from the conversation of several persons at the soiree, but it had no effect upon him. She knew *he* was rich, independent of his father; for his deceased uncle, Fairfield Buckingham, had left him a large plantation in Georgia, with many valuable slaves.

Our hero, you can easily believe, was a frequent visitor at No. — La Fayette Place, always to Julia a welcome intruder, for she had become much interested in the young Southerner, who soon discovered that her intellect was of the first order, and consequently became every day deeper enthralled. Her father had prided himself on giving her the best education in his power; he would not send her to boarding school, for he believed that the learning usually obtained at such places was merely superficial. So tutors were provided her at home, and she became a model in every respect. This Eugene learned, partly from herself and partly from his own observations, which were generally pretty correct.

But, however pleased the fair Julia might have been with her lover, Dr. Tennyson evidently disliked his visits, when he found they had an object. As a friend and social companion he thought well of him, but he was determined his danghter should never be united to a slave-holder, and for this reason alone he did not wish her to encourage him.

Miss Tennyson, among her other accomplishments, included that healthful one of riding on horseback, and certainly was a most fearless and graceful rider; at any rate, so Eugene thought as he accompanied her one fine afternoon to Bloomingdale. She rode on that occasion a beautiful cream-colored pony, with a mane and tail as white as ocean's foam, a spirited animal that cantered along as if proud of its precious burden. If Eugene thought Julia charming at other times, he considered her perfectly enchanting now, in her elegant riding costume; for he thought as most gentlemen do, that a lady, especially if she be young and well-formed, never appears to such advantage as on horseback, provided she is a graceful rider.

One morning Buckingham called in a carriage to invite Miss Tennyson to accompany him to Greenwood Cemetery. She accepted and was tripping down stairs to go, when the Doctor called her to him from the back parlor.

"My child," said he, "where are you going?"

"To ride in the country with Mr. Buckingham."

"Julia; I have told you before, not to encourage this young man. I do not wish it—his principles don't suit me. You must give up his society. Will you obey me or not?"

Julia blushed deeply and held down her head, but replied, "I will not go with him after to-day, father."

"See that you do not then."

This conversation was unintentionally overheard by Eugene, who was standing in the street door waiting for Miss Tennyson, and it sent a thrill of disappointment through his heart. At the moment he felt utterly wretched, and as he handed Julia into the carriage and took a seat by her side, he sighed bitterly. She looked at him but said nothing, and then rested a shade of melancholy on her own fair cheek.

After what had passed, it was not surprising that the young people labored under a mutual embarrassment during the drive to Greenwood; and while they were wandering through its rural labyrynths. As they walked on, admiring the lovely flowers and ornamental trees, and reading the sweet and touching inscriptions on the numerous, chaste, and elegant monuments, Eugene's eyes expressed deep sadness; he sighed frequently, and was evidently so preoccupied, that Julia asked what ailed him. He replied that he felt a little indisposed; but the truth was, he was endeavoring to make up his mind to leave New-York, and banish himself from the charmer at his side, and after a long struggle with himself, decided to do so.

In the meantime their steps brought them to a spot where several little tomb-stones raised their marble faces from the bright green grass around them.

"Is not that beautiful?" exclaimed Julia, as she read their simple inscriptions. "'Sweet little Charley'—'our baby'—'dear William'—'our angel boy.' And farther on, 'my mother.' Here Julia could not repress her tears, for her own mother had only been dead about two years: and Eugene led her away without speaking, till they came to the most splendid piece of sculpture in the Cemetery. This was a monument built in the form of a church, with a door in front, in which stood the marble figure of a lovely young girl in ball-room attire. "Strange idea!" exclaimed Eugene, "to dress the dead thus."

"Do not judge too hastily," said Julia; "after you have fully examined the beauty of this elegant mausoleum. I will relate to you the history of the fair girl who is here buried."

Eugene stood for half an hour in silent contemplation of the tomb of Charlotte Canda. He could not cease to admire the beauty of the structure, the tasteful ornaments surrounding it, the marble flower-pots in which were planted rare flowers, the two angels, large as life, placed in either side of the tomb, as if guarding it from every intruder, and the tasteful manner in which flowers were placed around the inner side of a neat iron railing surrounding the monument.

In the meantime, Julia had seated herself on a bench beneath the shade of a large oak tree, and Eugene having finished his survey, came and took a seat beside her.

"Charlotte Canda," began the fair girl, "was the only daughter of a rich French gentleman, who was the superintendant of a large and successful Seminary in New-York. This young lady was mistress of every accomplishment, and the idolized of her parents. Beautiful and wealthy, she was surrounded by suitors, and no ball or party among her acquaintances was considered complete without her presence.

"It was on her birth-night, when she had attained her seventeenth year, that she spent the evening from home, accompanied by her father, in her rich ball dress; she never looked more beautiful, and her friends remarked that she never was so happy and joyous.

"It was late when they set out to return home, and as they stopped on the way to leave a lady, Mr. Canda having gone to wait on her to the door, the coachman negligently dropped the lines, and the horses started off on a run. As they turned the corner, Miss Canda fell through the open door upon the side walk, and was so injured that she never spoke after.

"It was said that the monument was designed by herself for a beloved aunt, who lies with her in the same spot. The grief of her parents none but parents can imagine; and her death cast a gloom upon the whole circle of her acquaintance."

"A melancholy story, indeed," sighed Eugene, as they rose and walked on. The sun was now declining, and they entered their carriage to return. It was nearly dark when they arrived at her father's dwelling, and on parting with Miss Tennyson, Buckingham pressed her hand while he observed, "I omitted to mention that I am obliged to leave for home tomorrow; as I have received a letter from my father insisting on my immediate return—(this was true,) and I hope when I again visit the city, you will permit me to call on you."

Julia was both surprised and embarrassed. She became quite pale, and stammered forth—"Is it possible? I—I am sorry—I mean—I regret that you go so soon."

Then Eugene, much agitated drew from his coat pocket his daguerreotype, saying, "In the meantime, will you condescend to accept this?"

Julia started, hesitated, and at last replied "Not *now*." Then after a moment, "but I shall be happy to see you when you return."

And thus they parted.

As Buckingham, after leaving his horse at the livery stable, walked slowly down Broadway to the Astor, he mused thus: "'Not *now!*' that surely means that she will accept it sometime. She evidently regards me favorably—and in time she will consent to be mine. *Mine!* will that glorious presentiment of my life be ever realized? Yet, she said, '*not now*,' and these two short words shall be the talisman upon which my hopes are centred."

At this moment a hand was laid upon his shoulder, and a voice exclaimed, "I say, Buckingham, what are you thinking about? I have been walking beside you these ten minutes and you never saw me."

Eugene started from his reverie and colored deeply as Arlington Melville looked closely in his face. "I was thinking," he replied,

"Of course—but on what subject? So, it is a secret?"

Our hero to evade the question, replied, "I am going home to-morrow."

"Oh! To the South. That is a place I have often desired to visit, said the other, "I have heard a great deal about planters and slaves, and should like to make my own observations. I think I will go sometime."

"Why not now?" quickly exclaimed Eugene. "Come with me, you have nothing to prevent you. I should be most happy to introduce you to my father and sister."

"Sister, have you a sister? Well, let me see. When do you go?"

"To-morrow."

The young man mused for a few moments. Then shaking Eugene by the hand, he exclaimed—"I will go—many thanks for your invitation. Good bye, till to-morrow!" And he ran into the Irving House, leaving his friend to continue his walk alone.

Arlington Melville was a cousin of Julia's; and had just arrived from England, where his parents still resided. Although Eugene had often met him at Dr. Tennyson's house, where he seemed perfectly at home, he boarded at the Irving. Buckingham liked him much, especially as he saw plainly that he was no rival in the affections of the beautiful Julia, with whom his friendship was only a cousinly regard. Young, handsome and gay, with an educated mind, and heir to a considerable property in England, he was calculated to win admiration and esteem from all his acquaintance. Therefore Eugene was much pleased at the idea of his company on his journey home.

CHAPTER IV.

> "To die is to be banished from myself;
> "And Julia is myself; banished from her,
> "Is self from self, a deadly banishment."—*Shakspeare.*
>
> "And though the slave be fettered in the flesh,
> "He doth not feel his chains."—*Tupper.*

Buckingham and his young friend arrived at the dwelling of the former on the last day of June. They received a warm welcome from the Colonel and the fair Cora, who made a deep impression upon the heart of Melville. Her soft languid eyes, and her gentleness of demeanor, quite fascinated him.

Eugene had much to tell regarding his adventures in the North, nor was he long silent concerning the lovely Julia. Saying little in regard to his love for her, he related to his father and sister the whole history of his romantic acquaintance with the accomplished Miss Tennyson. After hearing him out, the old gentleman declared that if he had any idea of marrying her, he would banish him both from home and affection. "She is a portionless girl," said he;

"besides, Engene, you are well aware of my justly grounded prejudices against the Northerners, chiefly on account of their abolitionism, and their interference with our slaves. Although many of our neighbors have sent their sons to Northern colleges, I was determined you should not enter one; and if I had known of your projected visit to New-York, I should certainly have prevented it. Therefore, banish any ideas regarding a connection in that quarter, I will never listen to them."

Eugene, as usual, made no reply, but was just as determined as before to think of none but Julia. Although forbidden to address her, both by her father and his, he had a secret presentiment that she alone was to be his earthly partner, and as,

'Hope springs eternal in the human breast,"

he felt for the time being almost content. In the meanwhile, he considered that Julia might become engaged to another during his absence; that he had given her no proof of his affection, although he felt confident that she preferred him; and that it was necessary, perhaps, for the happiness of both, that he should declare his passion. Therefore, on the anniversary of "our Glorious Independence," he penned her the following delectable epistle:

"*Buckingham Hall, July 4th,* 18—.

"DEAR MISS TENNYSON,

"I have no doubt you will be surprised on receiving this epistle from me; yet I hope you will pardon the liberty I take, and excuse my presumption in addressing you; which I trust you will, for you know that Cupid has neither patience nor prudence.

"This letter is dated on the 'Glorious Fourth,' a day which brings to our remembrance the immortal 'Declaration of Independence,' and I think that it may very appropriately be used for *other declarations;* therefore I have decided to make one of these to you, and in the language of one of the illustrious signers of that immortal document, 'sink or swim, survive or perish, live or die,' I give my *heart* and *hand* to this declaration.

"You will perhaps consider me premature in this matter, but *dear lady!* if you know anything of the exquisite pangs of love, you will not think so. I hope you will not sacrifice me *now*, whem I am just beginning to live. No! you could not be so cruel.

"As the wound I have received from the little 'blind archer' has nearly proved mortal, *you only* can prevent my dissolution. For *heaven's sake!* dear lady! have pity on me; heal this wound and put me out of misery. The fact is, I can neither read, write, study, or do anything else as I ought, for my mind reverts incessantly to you, *you* are the theme of my meditations by night and by day.

"I confess I am not worthy of your varied charms, but I will endeavor to make myself more so; and may that Great Being, in whose hands are held our destinies, influence you to decide in my favor.

"I shall await your answer in *anxious suspense.* In the meantime I remain,

"Yours devotedly,

"EUGENE BUCKINGHAM."

In the course of a fortnight he received a reply, indefinite indeed, but which allowed him to hope. In the meanwhile he had written to her father as follows:

"HONORED SIR,

"As I received, when at your hospitable dwelling many tokens of friendship and esteem from you, I was emboldened, perhaps with too much assurance, to place my affections on your matchless daughter. No, I am wrong, I loved her *years* ago, before I was allowed the delight of gazing upon her in reality. She has long been my *ideal* and my *idol*, and the one *great presentiment* of my life is, and has been, that *we are to be united.*

"May I hope that you will not scorn my alliance? That you will one day allow me to call you by the endearing name of 'father?' Should you, however, entertain any prejudices against my Southern education, let me know them, and I will endeavor to convince you that they are not well founded.

"I will refer you to Gen. P. of Charleston, one of our first men, for any information you may require concerning my character and standing in this community.

"Trusting that you will pardon my presumption, I subscribe myself,

"Your humble servant,

"EUGENE BUCKINGHAM."

After some time our hero received the following reply:

"MR. BUCKINGHAM, SIR,

"According to your request, I wrote to Gen. P. and have just received his answer. He gives you a fair character, and intimates that your standing is good. He also says that you are quite wealthy, and own a plantation in Georgia, *well stocked with slaves.*

"Now, sir, to be candid with you, I will say, that from what I have seen and heard, I entertain, personally, a high opinion of you; but, sir; I have one great objection to urge against your suit; that is, you are *too rich*, you own *too much stock;* and I never can consent to suffer *my* daughter to marry a *slave-holder*, a man who engages in that *horrid traffic* of buying and selling *human flesh and blood*, and treating his fellow men as brutes.

"I have no more to say, you have my answer.

"Yours, &c.

"J. M. TENNYSON."

On reading this epistle Eugene's hopes fell below zero; but on reflection, and remembering that his motto was "Perseverance," he concluded to write again to the Doctor, in order to remove; if he could, some of his unjust opinions of slave-holders. Therefore he penned the following:

"DR. TENNYSON, RESPECTED SIR,

"I take the liberty of again addressing you, in order, if possible, to remove some of your erroneous ideas regarding slavery and slave-holders. I find the generality of the Northerners are prejudiced against us, but I suppose one reason of this is, because they have been accustomed to look on the *dark* side of the question, in every respect. You, yourself, perhaps, have never given the bright side an hour's thought: no doubt you have been much engaged in reading works against slavery, or listening to some free-soiler or abolitionist who exaggerates the evils of it in the highest terms. If you were to visit the South, and travel through it with an unprejudiced mind, your ideas in regard to the 'evils of slavery' would be much changed; you would find that we are not the inhuman monsters the abolitionists represent us to be. You might occasionally come across a hard master, but, as a general thing, the slaves are treated kindly; for if a planter was even disposed to treat them otherwise, public opinion would compel him to use them well.

"As for 'treating them like brutes,' I can assure you it is a slander of our enemies—I have not seen a grown slave whipped for years—and as to working them hard: when we task them, they generally get through in half a day, so that they are not obliged to do more than a common day's work in two days. When they get sick they are always allowed a physician, and are much better fed and clothed than any free negroes around them. In fact, they regard the latter with contempt, and say that 'they pity the poor nigger that has no master to take care of him.' I think you would also find them much more contented and happy than many of your Northern colored people.

"Some of your States have already passed laws prohibiting *free* negroes from settling within their borders; in others, they are not permitted to give evidence in courts of justice, or even to send their children to the same school with the whites, so that where the former are not numerous enough to form a school by themselves, they are obliged to remain in ignorance. You will not, if you can avoid it, even ride in the same conveyance with them; in short, notwithstanding the outcry against slavery, your free blacks are used with more tyranny and contempt than any of our slaves; for *we* never send them to poor-houses or suffer them to beg about the streets. On the whole, I think it is a mistake to suppose that slavery has been abolished in the North, as your negroes are subjected to the most humiliating of slaveries, universal tyranny of prejudice; they may be said, indeed, to be as they really are, *masterless slaves.*

"'See that there be not a beam in thine own eye, before thou attemptest to pull the mote out of thy brother's,' might be applied to some of your philanthropists. I have often thought, that if George Thomson, M. P. the celebrated English abolitionist, had devoted as much of his time and energy towards ameliorating the condition of the *poor white slaves* of England, as he has in travelling through our country, producing agitation between the North and South, in his vain attempt to cause the emancipation of *our* slaves, he would have gained more credit for himself and country, and done more good for the cause of *suffering humanity.* It is a well known fact that in the manufacturing and mining districts of England, (especially the latter,) the poor are obliged to endure more hardships than we can imagine. There are men working in some of the mines who have rarely beheld the light of day, there have they been brought into the world, and there, without education of any kind, have they been obliged to work, some of them harnessed, like dogs, to a cart, and crawling on their hands and feet through the dismal chambers of these damp caverns, till an early death terminates their miserable existence. O shame, where is thy blush? Can it be possible that such things are suffered in the nineteenth century? And by the very people, too, who presume to lecture us on the treatment of *our* slaves! The two subjects should not be mentioned on the same day—no, not even in the same year.

"Did ever a Southerner use his slaves as the ancient Romans are said to have done? which was, to place those who were either superannuated or sickly, upon an Island of the Tiber to *starve.* It was a professed maxim of the elder Cato to sell his worn-out slaves at any price, rather than maintain what he considered a useless burden. *We* on the contrary, think that we cannot render too many comforts to our old and faithful servants, whose condition, as Demosthenes said of the Athenian slaves, is far better than that of their free brethren.

"If your Northern men were to possess themselves of correct information regarding slavery and slaveholders, they would have a better opinion of us; instead of swallowing down, without digestion, the vile denunciations of ultra-abolitionists and political demagogues, men who have *not* the good of the colored man at heart, but who make the slavery question their *hobby*, with the vain expectation of riding into power thereon: agitators, who, to gain their ends, would *jeopardise* the very *existence* of our 'Glorious Union,' that noble structure which has been reared by the most skilful architects, and repaired and preserved by the most finished workmen. Yet these demagogues, like the Ephesian Erostratus, who fired the Temple of Diana solely to acquire *fame*, would not scruple to apply the *sacrilegious torch* to *our* mighty Temple of Liberty, merely to gratify their foolish and criminal love of notority. *Their* thirst for power is so great that they would sooner 'rule in Hell than serve in Heaven.' God forbid that they should succeed in their infernal designs, or that our glorious republic should commit suicide.

"Is that difficult problem, 'whether man is capable

of self government, or can a republic be permament,' *now* to be solved? and will the solution be, that after a fair trial of three-quarters of a century, the republic of the United States was dissolved in bloodshed, anarchy and chaos? Methinks at such a catastrophe the Goddess of Liberty would cover her face with her mantle, and shed *tears of blood* over the wreck of her *model Republic.*

"Such a state of things would undoubtedly be produced if the schemes of these Northern and Southern agitators were carried out.

'Men who, living, forfeit all renown,
'And doubly dying, shall go down
'To the vile dust from whence they sprung,
'Unwept, unhonoured and un-*hung.*'

"But I hope the wisdom of those *true Patriots*, the *Union men*, will prevail, as I trust that Heaven has ordained that our Republic shall last 'till time shall be no more.'

'Sail on, sail on, O ship of state,
Sail on, O Union strong and great,
Humanity with all its fears,
With all its hopes of future years,
Is hanging breathless on thy fate.

'We know what masters laid thy keel,
What workmen wrought thy ribs of steel,
Who made each mast and sail and rope
What anvils rung, what hammers beat,
In what a forge, in what a heat
Were shaped the anchors of thy hope.'

"You see, sir, that I am a *Union man*, although I *do* hail from the Nullification State, and that I abhor, from the depth of my heart, agitators and dis-unionists, whether they belong either to the North or South.

"Pardon this long epistle, and believe me to be

"Yours, most respectfully,

"E. BUCKINGHAM."

To this he received the answer that follows:

"MR. BUCKINGHAM, SIR,

"I must confess you have enlightened me on some points in regard to the treatment of slaves; as you judged rightly in supposing that I had never travelled through the South for the purpose of studying the workings of the system; but you have *not* made a *convert* of me *yet.* I am as confident as ever that the system is wrong in the main, for is it not contrary to scripture, to nature, and to common humanity? The Bible commands us to 'love our neighbor as ourselves,' to 'do unto others as we would have them do unto us;' and how can any man fulfil this scheme of universal benevolence who holds an unfortunate person captive against his will? who brings him down to the most insupportable of human conditions? who considers him his private property, and treats him, not as a fellow being, nor as one of the same common parentage as himself, but as an animal of the brute creation?

"Another objection to the system is, that the Scripture assures us of future rewards and punishments—and how can that man be called to an account for his actions when these actions are not at his own disposal? This strikes at the very root of slavery, and shows conclusively that the system is incompatible with the Christian religion. It is also contrary to our civil law; and we acknowledge in almost the first sentence of that immortal document, the Declaration of Independence, 'that *all* men are born free and equal,' while we have practised a *living lie* ever since that axiom was given to the world; and how much longer we shall be guilty of it, Heaven only knows. To suit our practice, *that part* of the Declaration should have read thus: 'All men are born free and equal—*except negroes*.'

"The only way we can rid ourselves of the reproach continually cast upon us by other nations, will be for slave-holders to emancipate their slaves and send them to Liberia.

"But, I have said enough to convince you that I hold the *same opinions* that I did when I first wrote to you.

"Yours truly,

"J. M. TENNYSON."

To this Eugene again made reply:

"DR. TENNYSON, DEAR SIR,

"Your letter has created hopes within me that you

are under conviction, but do not want to acknowledge it. It has actuated me to address you again.

"I cannot agree with you that slavery is condemned in Scripture—as we find it mentioned in many parts of the sacred volume, without any disapproval.

"We read of the existence of slavery soon after the deluge. Abraham obtained the favor of the Lord because he commanded his children and household after him, to do the will of God. Egypt was a market for slaves, (See the history of Joseph,) and Homer mentions Cyprus and Egypt as slave-markets at the time of the Trojan war. Tyre and Sidon were noted for the traffic. Joel, 3: 3, 4, 6. The Scripture also commands servants to obey their masters. Eph. 6: 5, 6, 7, 8. And St. Paul, after converting Onesimus to the Christian faith, sent him back to his master Philemon, from whom he had been a fugitive slave. So that slavery was not formally prohibited by the Bible.

"As to the argument concerning future rewards and punishments, that you lay so much stress upon, and say that it 'strikes at the very root of slavery, and shows conclusively that the system is contrary to Scripture;' allow me to say, that this is a palpable sophism; for, as the slave is *not* a free agent, his master compelling him to act *his* pleasure, the master, and *not* the slave, is accountable for those actions.

"Paley says, 'a man is said to be obliged, when

he is urged by a violent motive resulting from the command of another.' The violent motive with the slave is the command of his master, coupled with the fear of punishment, and with the soldier to obey his commander; hence, it is evident that the master in the one case, and the commander in the other, assumes the responsibility both to God and man, of the actions of the men who are compelled to obey them.

"You say that slavery is contrary to civil law—but Justinian remarks, that civil law gives nations the power to *make slaves*, and Paley tells us that the law of nature allows slavery to arise from three causes—1st. from crimes, 2d. from captivity, 3d. from debt; and we read also in history that the Helots became the slaves of the Spartans merely from the right of conquest.

"But, in whatever way slavery may have originated, it was practised almost universally from the earliest ages up to the close of the twelfth century, when it was suppressed in Europe, but about the time of the discovery of the American continent the African slave-trade was commenced again by the Portuguese, and other nations followed their example. The system was continued until the beginning of the present century, when it was abolished by law in America, England and France, and many other of the European nations. At present there are comparatively few slaves brought from Africa; and those few are smuggled into Cuba, or some of the South American provinces. This is a concise history of slavery.

"No man can be more opposed to the African slave-trade than I; and I also dislike the internal traffic as it is carried on in our Southern States. Slave-dealers there are held in contempt by all honorable men. But this system will continue as long as Virginia, Maryland and North Carolina remain as slave states, as a great portion of those states are worn out, and will not grow cotton, tobacco and other produce. Consequently, the inhabitants find it more profitable to breed slaves to supply the other States, and stock the new slave territory.

"But what would you have us do with our slaves? Would you have us emancipate them at once, and throw them upon the tender mercies of the world? This would never do, as most of them know nothing about business, and could never make a living for themselves if they were free; they would only be a nuisance to the country. But do not suppose we all maintain slavery from choice, far from it, as some of us are slave-holders from compulsion, (as you will learn in the sequel,) and would gladly get rid of our slaves if we could, as they cost us more than free labor. Should the crops fail, some of the planters are nearly eaten out of house and home by their numerous slaves.

"You mention Colonization: of having them sent to Liberia, but, sir, this is out of the question; for, at the rate the Colonization Society have been shipping them off for the last thirty years, we would never get clear of the system. During that time there have only been about seven thousand colonized. We might as well attempt to clear one of our large forests by cutting down a tree every year, for while we are making the removal, thousands are growing up instead. Yet, should all the slaves be emancipated, the expense of sending so many to such a distance could not be incurred. Still, I am in favor of Colonization, but not on account of its vain endeavors to abolish slavery. I am in favor of it because it spreads the Christian religion and civilization among the millions of ignorant natives in Africa.

"It is evident, from the increase of our slave population, that to get rid of the system, we must adopt some more feasible plan than that of Colonizing them in Africa, as it is estimated that at the present ratio of increase, said population would amount to twelve millions at the close of the present century.

"My plan to abolish slavery would be for Government to purchase Cuba, or else to appropriate a large part of our Southern Territory, either in Utah or New Mexico for the purpose of Colonization. If this plan was carried out, and your Northern fanatics and agitators were to let us alone, in a few years you would hear of one State after another declaring itself free. Had not these men interfered with our institutions, Kentucky and Virginia would have been free states before this time.

'Very Respectfully,

"E. BUCKINGHAM."

The next letter from Dr. Tennyson concluded the correspondence.

"MR. BUCKINGHAM, SIR,

"You accuse me in your last letter of advancing sophistical arguments, but, I think *that* accusation would more appropriately apply to your last epistle. In the first place, you wish to convey the idea that Abraham was commended by the Lord for owning slaves, but, sir, this is a palpable perversion of Scripture; as he was only praised because he commanded his 'children and household after him to keep in the way of the Lord.' You will observe that his children and servants are mentioned in connection; they were treated in many respects alike, they were circumcised alike by the command of the Lord, and they received the same moral and religious training. Could your masters of the present day receive the same commendation for the *moral* and *religious* training you give your slaves? I trow not.

"Another scriptural perversion: you say that St. Paul, after converting Onesimus to the Christian faith, sent him back to his master Philemon, from whom he had been a fugitive slave. But, sir, you cannot strain this passage to encourage the restoration of fugitive slaves, as the benevolent Apostle in his letter to Philemon, remarks farther on, 'I send him back to you, but not in his former capacity, not now a servant, but above a servant, a brother beloved.' So that Onesimus returned to Philemon not a slave, but a minister of the gospel, and afterwards became Bishop of Ephesus.

"It is true that the Scripture did not formally condemn or prohibit slavery, but the reason is obvious—slavery, at the time of the introduction of Christianity, was a part of the civil constitution of most countries; and if Christianity had abruptly declared that the millions of slaves should be made free, it would have been universally rejected as promulgating doctrines that were dangerous, if not destructive, to society; therefore it never meddled, by any positive precept, with the institutions of the times; for though it does not positively say, 'you shall neither buy nor sell, nor possess a slave,' it is evident from the mild diffusion of its light and influence, and from its general tenor, that it militates against the slavery system.

"Christianity brought about the abolition of slavery all over Europe about the close of the twelfth century; and through its influence slavery had declined in heroic Greece and papal Rome centuries before. It will also be the main cause of freeing the slave in our own country. God grant that period may soon arrive!

"This is the last letter I will address you on this subject, and I do not wish to receive any more from you, as it is evident that there is nothing to be gained by further correspondence.

"Yours, &c.

"J. M. TENNYSON."

CHAPTER V.

"The master of a well ordered household is kind to his servants, yet he exacteth reverence, and each one feareth at his post."

Tupper.

During Arlington Melville's stay with his friend, his time was principally employed riding about and visiting the surrounding country, sometimes accompanied by the Colonel; occasionally by Eugene, and oftener by Miss Buckingham, with whom the young Englishman had become almost as much in love as our hero was with Julia. Cora was certainly delighted with his society, and as her father made no objection, they were very often together, riding, walking, or sitting in a vine covered arbour at the farther end of the spacious garden, in the rear of the mansion; where, with books and music their time passed quickly and happily away. But Cora was always attended by Rosa, her favorite slave, who was a pretty light mulatto; and the presence of the girl prevented Melville from saying many tender things by way of declaring his passion. Yet his dark, eloquent eyes spoke plainly what his lips never whispered; and Cora understood, and replied in the same delightful language.

One day Eugene expressed his intention of visiting his Plantation in Georgia, and invited Melville to accompany him, which he willingly agreed to do. The young men therefore left Charleston in the morning train for Macon, Georgia, near which place was Fairfield Plantation, the domain of our hero. They arrived at Augusta the same evening, and immediately changed cars for Macon. While doing so Melville was much amused, as well as surprised, in watching the removal of a lot of slaves from one train to another. The reader must know that there are always a number of "stock cars" on these Southern railroads, attached to the end of the passenger train, for the purpose of freighting slaves. These cars are perfectly round, like a coal wagon, or looking like a large hogshead on wheels, yet capacious enough to hold near a hundred; and here the poor creatures are huddled together like so many pigs or cattle going to market, and when the weather is warm they suffer intensely from the heat and closeness of the cars.

Melville observed that there were several lots of slaves in these cars which had been bought in Virginia for the New Orleans market. It was in the dusk of the evening, and each trader or owner went round hunting up his own property, which was rather difficult to do, as he scarcely knew one from another. But the slaves knew their proper owner, and with a grin on their shining ebony faces, called out, "I 'longs to you, massa, I 'longs to you." While others would cry "I no 'longs to you, sir; I 'longs to dat oder man wid de red face and big whiskers."

At length the slaves were arranged to their masters' satisfaction if not to their own, and the cars started. Soon after, our friends began to doze in their comfortable seats, for the passenger cars were as well furnished as the others were miserable.

At the break of day some of the passengers were aroused by the car-agent, to look at a curiosity called Stone Mountain, near Atalanta, which was quite a resort for travellers. It rose in the shape of a pyramid, several hundred feet, on an open plain, and was ascended by a winding road. Half way up was situated an elegant hotel, and the top of the mountain was surmounted by a statue.

They soon left it behind, however, and as they passed onward various amusing and pleasant sights met their inquiring gaze. At length, in the course of the afternoon. Eugene and Arlington arrived at Macon, after which half an hour's ride brought them to Fairfield Plantation, which they had no sooner reached than dozens of slaves young and old ran out of the house, with the greatest appearance of delight, to welcome their young master. Eugene shook hands with many of them, and spoke kindly and frankly to the others.

After a slight refection, the young men went forth to survey the premises. As they passed along in the rear of the mansion, Melville noticed with much pleasure the neatness of the out-buildings and the rural appearance of the white-washed cabins, in which resided the most of the slaves. They were surrounded by flowers and creeping plants, and in a little garden attached to each were vegetables and herbs. There were plenty of chickens and other poultry running about: and Melville thought that the numerous cabins placed in rows at the rear of the large house, gave the place the appearance of a little town.

"One would imagine," said he, "that these creatures were happy, with so many little comforts; but I never can believe that a *slave can* be happy."

"They *are* happy," replied his friend. "You see these little gardens and that poultry—well, these negroes, when their daily task is finished, cultivate their vegetables and attend to their poultry until they are fit for market, and then they will sell, for a good price, either to the family of their master or other persons, their little stock of produce. The money thus gained is spent by them and their families in purchasing gay clothing and trinkets, of which they are particularly fond. So you see they are allowed many privileges which not only render them more contented with their lot, but naturally cause them to be greatly attached to their master or mistress."

As the young men walked on, the little woolly headed blacks peeped timidly out at them from behind the garden palings, and as they approached them, would run away giggling and chattering like so many parrots. Melville could not help laughing at the drollery of their looks, half naked as they were, and observed—" These little fellows seem happy enough."

" Why should they not? They have nothing to do. Children are never tasked until they are ten or twelve years old."

After they had finished their survey of the habitations, the young men extended their walk to the cotton and rice fields, which were in a high state of cultivation. Here several slaves were yet at work pulling cotton, one of the overseers standing near with a whip in his hand, which however was seldom used in this well-ordered plantation. When the poor creatures saw Eugene their joy was expressed in loud shouts of delight. He spoke to them all, and directed the overseer to let them go home. After they had gone, the friends continued their ramble. They passed along large fields of cotton, tobacco, and rice, all presenting a flourishing aspect, and on their return rested awhile in a lovely grove of palmettos, whose glossy, fan-like leaves hung gracefully down, and were gently swayed to and fro by the evening breeze.

"I cannot help pitying these poor negroes," said Melville, "although I see that they are kindly treated by their master. Poor, ignorant creatures! they are obliged to work day after day with a whip at their backs, and receive nothing in return but their simple food and scanty supply of clothing."

"What need have they of any thing else?" rejoined Eugene, "they are clothed warmly enough for the climate, they have enough to eat, and they are as happy as ignorance can be. We use them kindly, and yet we must keep them under our control, we *must* keep them in fear; for should their natural tiger-like disposition get the upper hand, it would be *death* to the planter."

"How can that be?" inquired Melville, "when they evidently love their master with all the simplicity of their nature. Surely they could not harm *him.* Were he a cruel, hard-hearted man, such as I have several times seen among the Planters in your native

State, it would not be surprising that they should wish to rid themselves and the world of a monster. But not a master such as your father and yourself."

Eugene smiled. "If those Northern abolitionists were to stop their meddling in our concerns, the condition of the slaves would be much improved. They come among us as friends—and while enjoying our hospitality, whisper sedition and conspiracy into the ears of our slaves, and often go so far as to steal them from us. If they were to let us alone, there is no doubt that, in the course of years, not a slave State would be in existence; and for my part I should rejoice to see that time arrive. If I could, I would this moment emancipate every one of *my stock*, but unfortunately for *my happiness*, they are all entailed to me and my posterity by my uncle, who died a couple of years since."

"I am surprised to hear you talk thus, my dear Buckingham. *Your happiness?* what has that to do with possessing *stock*, as you call it?"

Eugene seemed somewhat confused, and did not reply immediately. At last he said, "My dear friend, I might as well confide in you, as you have an interest in the lovely being who is the day star of my existence." Then, as Melville listened, surprise gathering on his handsome countenance, our hero related to him the story of his life, his love and his disappointment. When he had finished there was a long silence between the friends. At length Melville broke through it by exclaiming, "I too have a confession to make. Listen, Eugene! I—my dear friend —I love your sweet sister Cora."

"You love my sister!" cried the other much surprised, "and does she return your love?"

"I think so—I believe so—but I am not sure. I have never had an opportunity of declaring myself, because, (and this I consider one of the evils of slavery,) she is eternally attended by a little black girl who watches me continually with a pair of great rolling eyes, as if she had strong suspicions that I intended to steal away her mistress."

Eugene could not help smiling, but he promised his friend that he should have *his* countenance in the matter if he was sure that his sister returned the young man's affection. After further conversation they returned to the mansion, where they found an excellent supper prepared for them.

When they had finished their meal, the young men took their station on a settee out on the veranda, to smoke a segar or two. For a while there was an unbroken silence between them, each being absorbed in his own reflections. The moon was very bright, although often obscured by fleeting clouds, and the night was a cool and pleasant one.

"Well," observed Melville at last, throwing away what remained of his segar, "I must confess I have been greatly edified this day, and very much amused too."

"I was just thinking," rejoined his companion, puffing out a volume of smoke, "that I could tell you a story to amuse you. Shall I? or are you amused enough? Take another segar?"

"No. What's the story? Come."

"It is about a capital joke played off upon one of the Northern abolitionists by some of our Charleston wags."

"Very well—go on."

Eugene leaned back on his seat, took his segar from his mouth, and began: "About two years ago an ultra-abolitionist from Syracuse, New-York, came to the city of Charleston on some business. His name was Harford, and he remained some time in our city. Being very much in awe of Judge Lynch, this man kept his ideas on slavery to himself, except when he chanced to meet with a 'kindred spirit,' and then his denunciations against slavery and slave-holders were frightful indeed. Among other strange whims he declared that he would never speak to, or touch the person of a slave while he stayed in Charleston, and that he would not taste a morsel of bread or any other thing that had, to his knowledge, been made or cooked by a slave.

"He stayed at the Planter's Hotel, and was in the habit of attending St. Philip's Church near by. The true reason of his devoutness was this: he had been very much taken by a beautiful young lady who was a constant attendant at the church. She was always richly and fashionably dressed, had lovely black eyes and long raven curls, and a form of exquisite symmetry.

"By inquiry he found that she was a milliner, and resided in the city. One of his Southern acquaintances, a complete wag, by the by, who was well acquainted with her, undertook to introduce the young man to this idol of his affections. It was done; and as Harford was a personable fellow, with a pretty good address, he found that he daily gained favor in her eyes.

"Several other young men got wind of it, and doing all they could to help the matter onward, soon had the delight of seeing the abolitionist married to the beautiful—*slave*."

"Slave!" echoed Melville, "ha! ha! ha! a capital joke that. Did the fellow find it out?"

"You shall hear. As soon as the rogues had them fast married, and in the midst of their honeymoon, they let out the secret, giving him undeniable proof of her being a slave, set up in business by her owners, who resided in the country, to whom her profits were regularly given.

"The fact is, any body unused to slaves, would be mistaken in some of them; they are so white. The only way to distinguish a slave from a white person, as I should say, to prove the existence of negro blood in the veins, is by examining the finger nails: the white crescent at the root in us, being wanting in them."

"That's a new idea!" cried Arlington, "if I were not an Englishman I would examine my own, that is, if there was light enough."

"Do you mean to insinuate, Mr. Melville," said Eugene rather haughtily, "that we Americans are all somewhat tainted?"

"Excuse me, my dear friend, I had no such intention. But do go on—how did the abolitionist get over his disappointment?"

"He never got over it. As a marriage with a slave is not legal, he was at liberty to leave her at any moment, yet he was so tormented and crowed over by those who knew his real sentiments, that mortified and crestfallen, he suddenly and privately escaped from the city, never to return."

As it was growing late, and the young men were weary with their journey, they soon retired to their respective rooms, and in a little while silence reigned over the whole household.

One pleasant morning the young friends, while strolling over a part of Fairfield Plantation, where the slaves were at work, observed some of them at the other side of a thick hedge; and overhearing their names mentioned, stopped to listen to the conversation.

"Who dat massa Mervil?" said one big fellow called Jeff.

"Dun you know?" retorted uncle Pete, an old gray headed negro; "he be de friend o' massa Eugene. Nice young gemmen too—he give ole nigger dollar toder day."

"What fur he give you dollar, I wan' to know?" cried a mulatto boy at a little distance.

"Caze I catch him fine large squirrel, all white. He say he want it for hansum missy."

"How you catch him? 'lucidate dat question! You can't run arter a cat," said the boy with a malicious grin.

Uncle Peter with a contemptuous look replied,—"My dog Jowler catch him, he fust rate at dat, I kin tell you."

Jeff now called out—"I say Uncle Pete! is you been do what you say?"

"What dat? I fogit what 'twas."

"Dah now! 'Pears like you fogit eberyting—you be grow so old. Didn't I tell you len' me dat possum dog to night, an' you say yes?"

"Well, sho' 'nough. But you don't wan' no dog to-night."

"What fur I don't?"

"Caze, you goin' to corn shuckin'."

"No I isn't. Why you say dat? I'se gwine to ketch possum for Polly."

"You big fool, Jeff!" cried uncle Peter disdainfully, "dun you know Polly aint goin' to hab you arter all you run arter her. She take all you gib her —she wear de nice tings, an' she eat up all de melons an' taters, an' eberyting. You let possum alone. Polly play you trick some ob dese days."

"How you know dat?" cried Jeff, looking much concerned.

"Caze, can't I see fur mysef. She too fond o' Car'lina Jake. Polly's a knowin' gal, I tell you."

"Dah now!' returned the other, "I don't beleibe a word o' dat; caze why, when I gib her bead necklace las' night, she tell me dat she lub me all ober."

Here there was a general cachinnation among the other slaves around, which our friends could hardly refrain from joining; but as they did not wish to be discovered, they were obliged to control themselves.

"Well, now," continued uncle Pete, "'pears like

P. 65 CHORUS. SING DARKEYS SING.

you haint got no sense. 'Taint no more dan yesterday dat I heard Car'lina Jake ax massa Eugene if he might hab a *fam'ly*, an' massa ax who 'twas, an' he said it was Polly."

Jeff's sable countenance fell below zero. "Dah now! aint dat too bad? Arter all I gib her dis whole year. Why, dis mornin' I make her beautiful present ob red hankercher. 'Pears like I neber hab no luck." And poor Jeff walked off with a very disconsolate air.

Eugene and his friend then continued their walk, laughing at the disappointment of the crestfallen lover, and coming to the conclusion that no station in life was too humble for the spirit of coquetry to flourish in.

That evening the "corn-shucking" or husking, came off. The corn was piled in large heaps before the row of cabins, and although it was a bright night, being the full of the moon, each little window of the slaves' habitations was illuminated by a couple of tallow candles, so that every object was distinctly visible.

Around the large corn heaps were seated over two hundred men and women, (many of whom were from the neighboring plantations,) tearing off the husks and throwing the ears into separate piles; and in the midst of their employment all were chattering, laughing, singing and telling stories, much to the amusement of themselves and the young gentlemen, who were seated a little apart observing the proceedings.

On the top of one of the heaps was mounted uncle Cato, one of the principle slaves, and a great favorite of Eugene's. He was noted for his talent of improvisation. He would sing one or more lines of a song and the chorus would be repeated by all the others. Some of the women had excellent voices, especially the coquet, Miss Polly, a pretty mulatto, who had Caroline Jake beside her, and who wore the identical scarlet handkerchief on her head in the form of a turban, smiling now and then on Jeff, who took no notice, but sat at a distance scowling defiance at his rival.

One of the songs ran thus:

"The lubly Moon it shine so brigl..,
We doesn't want no oder light,
Chorus: sing darkeys, sing!
De man up dare, he look at us,
He tink we make a great, big fuss,
Chorus: sing, darkeys, sing!
Possum-dog he cotch a coon,
Nigger skin him pretty soon,
Chorus: sing, darkeys, sing!
Sold de skin and got de chink,
Berry sorry dat I drink.
Chorus: sing, darkeys, sing!"

After this, whiskey was handed about by the

overseers, and the slaves becoming very merry, began to caper and sing more noisily than before.

" Massa Eugene hab good whiskey,
Makes de niggers bery friskey,
    Chorus: shucking ob de corn.
O, ho! de niggers jolly!
See dah, de pretty Polly!
    Chorus: Shucking ob de corn.
Dat ar Jake, he sits beside her,
Will she hab dat big black spider?
    Chorus: shucking ob de corn.
Jeff's so mad, he look like tunder—
O-o-o-o! who dat hit me wid de corn dah?
    Chorus: Jeff, he trew dat corn."

By this time the husking was finished, it being quite late, and as the song was concluded they all jumped up and had a regular break-down, exhibiting such ridiculous antics that Melville and Eugene laughed till they could laugh no longer from sheer exhaustion.

Then Buchingham ordered them to disperse and retire to their cabins; and the friends returning to the house, soon after sought their beds.

CHAPTER VI.

> " He says he loves my daughter;
> " I think so too: for never gazed the moon
> " Upon the water, as he'll stand and read,
> " As 'twere, my daughter's eyes."—*Shakspeare.*

After remaining at Fairfield Plantation about a week, during which time frequent rides and walks were taken by the young men around the adjacent country, Eugene thought it time to be returning home. On their departure the slaves assembled around them with evident regret at their going, and with one voice they cried, " God bless young massa, and soon bring him back."

They were soon seated in the cars and whizzing rapidly towards home. On the road Melville observed many interesting objects that had before escaped his notice; among other things the Spanish moss, as it is called, a singular production, growing in long waving tresses upon the trees of the forest, and appearing to derive its nourishment from the atmosphere alone, as it sends none of its fibers into the tree for sustenance. A small quantity taken from one tree and hung upon another, instead of dying from being torn from its first hold, will soon spread itself over the entire tree, and sending down from every branch a long waving streamer, as it were, gives the forest a dense and gloomy aspect which must be seen to be realized. This moss, in its prepared state, much resembles hair, is remarkably elastic, and is used in this country and exported to Europe for the manufacture of mattrasses.

About ten o'clock in the forenoon of the second day of their journey, something in the machinery of the locomotive got out of order, and the train was obliged to stop in the midst of a forest; many of the passengers left the cars, our friends among the rest. Here were about two dozen negroes employed in cutting timber. At least some of them were, and others lay about under the trees lazily enough, chattering, laughing and singing, (apparently perfectly happy,) such scraps as these:

> " Ole Virginny, neber tire—
> " Eat hog and hominy, and lie by de fire ;"

many of them composing their ditties extempore, without regard to rhyme or reason.

At length the machinery was put in order and

the train again started. In the course of the afternoon our friends reached Charleston, and in a little while stood on the veranda of Buckingham Hall, where Cora was the first to meet them, and her brother might easily divine, which he did, by the bright blush on her fair cheek, that her heart was lost to his friend. "Cora," said he, playfully patting her on the head, "you see I have brought him back safe. I suppose you have been lost without him for the past week."

Cora blushed still more deeply at these words, and looking up, met the speaking eyes of Arlington glowing upon her. Nothing was left her but to escape into the house, which she did with much more expedition than her natural indolence promised. The young men followed, and were soon joined by the Colonel, who inquired concerning the state of his son's plantation; and seemed well pleased with the favorable account Eugene gave of it.

That evening Cora told her brother that their father had invited F. Jones and his daughter to dine with them. With an exclamation of impatience, Eugene declared he would not stay in the house while the hated object remained there, but Cora assured him he would not be sorry if he yielded to his father's wishes in some respects. "Not that I wish you to marry her," continued the young girl, "but if you only show her a little countenance."

"A *very little* countenance indeed it will be," interrupted her brother; "but to please my father and you, I will consent for once to suffer the martyrdom of her presence."

Melville, who was near, smiled and observed, "I do not wonder at his dislike to Miss Jones, from what he has told me concerning her. It certainly must be a dreadful thing to be forced to marry one you hate, and be banished from the sweet society of *one you love.* Do you not think so, fair Cora?" There was a silvery sweetness in his voice, and a soft glow in his dark eyes, that went to the heart of the young girl, and she could but murmur—"I think so."

Eugene, thinking the time and place very meet for a declaration, and willing to do as he would wish to be done by, rose and left the room, taking with him little Rosa, the slave, on some pretence or other. Arlington looked around and understood his friend's manœuvre. Cora's eyes were bent upon an album in her lap as her lover again spoke in the same sweetly modulated tones. "So you think, fair girl, it is a sad thing to be banished, without a hope, from the side of the being you adore?"

Cora made no answer, but her head drooped lower over her album. He took her hand, and bending his knee before her like a lover of the olden time, continued—"if you think so, dearest, you cannot banish the suppliant at your feet, for he *loves you—adores you!* Have you the heart to banish me, sweet Cora?"

Cora opened her lustrous eyes and softly answered, "No!"

"Nor I either, I declare! I'm sure I could not!" laughed a voice behind him, as the delighted lover was in the act of raising her hand to his lips. Melville started to his feet, and Cora covered her face with her hands in deep confusion. The Colonel stood quietly in the middle of the room. The young man marched up to him with great resolution and accosted him thus: "Sir, have I your sanction?"

"You are a pretty fellow indeed! Is that the way you return my hospitality, by attempting to steal away my only daughter? There is no knowing what would have happened had I not entered the room, perhaps you would have had the audacity to kiss her."

"I think it very likely I should," boldly answered Melville.

"I must confess I think you have a good stock of impudence," said the Colonel, half laughing; "however. I forgive you, and as I chance to know something of youself and your relatives, I will not refuse my sanction."

The young man could scarcely find words to express his thanks, and Eugene, by this time making his appearance, was much gratified to see the course things had taken, yet could not repress a deep sigh at the thought of his own unhappiness.

The next day at noon, F. Jones, Esq. and his Amazon daughter made their appearance at the Hall. The Colonel gave them a warm reception, and Eugene a cold and stately one. As for Cora and Arlington, they were polite and attentive to the guests without being familiar. Our hero saw that his father's eye was upon him, and he made a desperate attempt to be civil to Miss Susanna Jones.

Before dinner the guests, accompanied by the Colonel and the rest, took a walk in the garden and grounds. Susanna had with her a little white poodle, of which she was extravagantly fond, and as they strolled along he was continually doing some mischief or other; either chasing the peacocks or running among the flowers and biting them from their stems. Col. Buckingham did not appear to notice him, but Cora, vexed to see her plants destroyed, caught up a switch and struck him; whereat Miss Jones exclaimed with passion, "How dare you strike my dog?"

Cora made no reply, but Arlington observed, "I think he deserves a little correction; Miss Buckingham's flowers are rare."

Susanna looked around as if surprised. "O, did he hurt the flowers? That was wrong. Here Diana," continued she, addressing her attendant slave, "take him and shut him up in the house, he deserves punishment, but I prefer to correct him myself," with an angry look at Cora, who, however, took no notice of it, but walked on, leaning on the arm of her lover, with her usual languid air.

This little incident, trifling as it was, indicated a trait in the character of Miss Jones that caused Eugene to dislike her more than ever. "What a wife she would make," he thought, "with her domineering passionate disposition."

At two in the afternoon dinner was announced. During the meal Eugene was silent and abstracted, while the rest were conversing with much vivacity. Miss Jones, who, by his father's management, was placed beside him, chattered in his ear like a magpie, although he scarcely gave her a word in return, notwithstanding he met the Colonel's angry eye upon him every time he glanced in that direction.

After dinner they repaired to the parlor, and Colonel Buckingham approaching his son and Susanna, who were looking over a portfolio of Cora's drawings, observed, "Did my daughter tell you, Miss Jones, of her engagement?"

"No, she did not," answered that lady with some surprise.

"There is the gentleman;" pointing to Melville, who was seated with Cora at one of the windows. "And I think," he continued in a jesting tone, "that we ought to have *another engagement* soon. What say you Eugene?"

Susanna put her fan before her face, and tried very hard to raise a blush, but she only looked tickled, while the young man, starting as if from a reverie, exclaimed, "Sir!"

His father gave him a glance that plainly said, "I am not to be trifled with," but Eugene cared not, he only waited to hear him speak.

"My respectable friend, Mr. Jones, has agreed with me that it would be a meet and advantageous thing for all parties, that the persons and fortunes of our children should be united. Therefore, as Miss Jones is not averse and Eugene *can not* be, I propose that the wedding come off by the latter end of next month."

"And I second that proposal," said Jones, advancing.

This scene would have made an excellent picture.

There stood the Colonel, tall and commanding, his arms folded, and his eyes bent sternly on his son—near him was Jones, a small, dark man, of insignificant appearance, looking on with a smirking countenance—his daughter Susanna close to our hero, her head turned aside and her handkerchief before her face, trying to look modest—in the back-ground Cora and Arlington looking up with much surprise on their countenances, and Eugene himself, his tall form drawn up to its full height, his dark eyes flashing, and every lineament of his countenance expressing anger and disdain.

Full two minutes passed before another word was spoken. Then Eugene, in a voice trembling with subdued passion, ejaculated—"Am I a *slave?* I *will not* submit to such *tyranny!* I *will not* be *forced* to marry against my will!" And as he spoke, he broke abruptly from their presence and was seen no more that day.

Jones sneaked into a corner, looking disappointed and foolish, while the elder Buckingham walked the floor with hasty strides, endeavoring to subdue the rising anger within him; and Susanna, after standing silent awhile, concluded to go into hysterics, and succeeded very well in frightening Cora and the young slaves. Melville, bursting with laughter, ran incontinently out of the house; and after indulging in merriment awhile, commenced singing as a *finale* to the performance,

"Oh, Susanna, don't you cry for me!"

CHAPTER VII.

"The wanderer was alone as heretofore:
"The beings which surrounded him were gone,
"Or were at war with him; he was a mark
"For blight and desolation."

After what had passed, Eugene was resolved again to quit his home, and in two days time found himself on his way to New-York, accompanied by Melville, whose private affairs obliged him to absent himself from his betrothed. Cora was very unhappy at the idea of his leaving her. "Perhaps," she sighed, "You will never return."

"Cruel girl!" was his reply, to harbor such a doubt.

Yet, their parting was one of love and regret; and when her brother in his turn, bade her adieu, there was a tear in his eye, which brought a shower to those of Cora. Eugene took no leave of his father, for the Colonel kept purposely aloof: and when the young friends stood together on the deck of the noble steamer, as she proudly sailed out of the beautiful bay of Charleston, there was a silent gloom enveloping the hearts of both.

The first day of their passage was calm and pleasant; but on the next night the rain fell in torrents and the sea was fearfully wrought; and to add to this, most of the passengers grew sea-sick, and then, as the boat ploughed through the rolling waves, there was *some heaving*. The Captain appeared to look upon it all as a joke, and called it only a salt water *breeze;* but the passengers learned from him next morning that he had been so much alarmed as to have the boats in readiness, expecting every minute, from the height of the gale, to see the pipes of the engine blow away. In a short time, however, the gale abated considerably, and our friends turned into their berths, resigning themselves to the kind care of Him who sayeth to the sea, "Be still!" and it obeyeth.

Nothing worthy of note occurred during the rest of the passage, and on arriving at the good city of Gotham the young men put up at the Astor, where Eugene met a warm reception from his former friend and host, Capt. Coleman. Very soon after his arrival, our hero, accompanied by Melville, paid a visit to the lovely Julia, who received them as each wished to be received, and for a short season Eugene felt happy in her presence. After an agreeable conversation, he took his leave; and her cousin then gave her a relation of his own adventures, and the trials and persecutions of his friend. If she was pleased with the first, she was much moved by the latter, and exclaimed several times, while drops glistened in her beautiful eyes, "Poor fellow! poor Eugene!"

The next day Buckingham called again, and finding his beloved alone, had a long conversation with her, during which he urged her to become his wife, and even ventured to propose an elopement. But Julia would not listen to such a proposal; she loved him, she said, but would not disobey her father.

"Gain his consent, dear Eugene, and I am yours. Not otherwise." But they parted as engaged lovers: he placed a diamond ring upon her finger, and they exchanged daguerreotypes.

Before he left the house, Buckingham resolved to press his suit once more with her father. He therefore sought him in his library. The Doctor correctly divined the subject the young man wished to enter upon, and inwardly resolved to be inflexible on the *one* point. After listening quietly until Eugene had exhausted all his rhotaric in endeavoring to soften his obdurate heart, the old Doctor replied, "If you will prove your love and devotion for my daughter, by emancipating your slaves, I will not refuse to grant my sanction to your mutual wishes—but, not until then."

"Would to God I could do it!" cried the young man with much emotion, "but it is impossible. They are entailed by the will of my uncle as long as Georgia shall remain a slave State."

Dr. Tennyson only replied, "Well sir, if that is the case, you have had my mind on the subject long ago. My opinions, like the laws of the Medes and Persians, are unchangeable. As long as you are a slave-holder you cannot marry my daughter with my consent."

Eugene was greatly affected by this reply. "O, sir!" he cried, "you cannot surely be so cruel as to make two human beings miserable by your prejudices—and one of them your only daughter. You know too, that I have the *will* but not the *power* to comply with your request, as I am the involuntary inheritor of this patrimony."

"Mr. Buckingham," said the Doctor, rising, "enough has been said on this subject. It is useless to waste any more words."

On this our hero took up his hat and with a formal "Good evening" took his departure, overwhelmed with disappointment and despair.

As he proceeded down Broadway, Eugene was plunged in melancholy reflections; and it was not until he had been sitting an hour or two in the gentleman's parlor at the Astor, that he recalled to mind his great presentiment—his belief that the destinies of himself and Julia were one day to be united. This thought caused him to shake off his despondency, and he began to form plans for future action, in the midst of which he was accosted by Arlington, who had just come in.

"Well, Eugene," he cried, taking a seat beside his friend, "how goes it with you now? Have you succeeded with the old gentlemen?"

"Indeed I have not," replied the other, sadly enough.

"I am sorry for you, sincerely I am. But what do you intend to do next? Are you going home?"

"No. To be persecuted again? What happiness, would I find *there?*"

"Will you stay here then?"

"I cannot—I must not. I shall travel. I must find change of scene and excitement. I will start for Niagara to-morrow, and proceed from thence by the lakes through the Western States. Will you accompany me?"

"I would with pleasure, but just now it is impossible, I have business in New-York that must be attended to. I could not go."

"I am sorry. Your society would be so acceptable."

Here the conversation of the young men was interrupted by an acquaintance of Melville's, with whom he had promised to go to the Broadway Theatre to hear Forrest. Arlington introduced him to Eugene, and after some words of ceremony, he joined with Melville in persuading our hero to accompany them.

The next morning Eugene prepared to leave the city without venturing again to visit La Fayette Place, even to bid farewell to his beautiful idol. The carriage was announced, his baggage secured, and accompanied by Melville, who wished to see him off, he proceeded to the wharf. The boat, which happened to be the Isaac Newton, one of the Hudson's floating palaces, was just ready to start. The friends shook hands warmly. "Remember me to Julia," said Eugene, while Arlington bid him be of good cheer, for he would assist him, with all his power, to attain the cherished wish of his heart.

It was on the morning of the first of October, 18—, that Eugene found himself rapidly gliding over the waters of one of the most beautiful rivers in America, and one whose scenery is unequalled. It was a day of unclouded splendor; and as our hero stood upon the deck, looking around him, his heart grew saddened, and he became absorbed in contemplation.

The month of October is calculated to engender melancholy reflections. The evidence of decay which

Nature exhibits in the fading and falling of her gorgeous drapery, is calculated to impress us with a sense of our own mortality—that we too, must soon become like the "sere and yellow leaf," and mingle with the clods of the valley—or as the Poet of the Seasons, says—

> "Pass some few years—
> Thy flowery Spring, thy Summer's ardent strength,
> Thy sober Autumn fading into age,
> And pale concluding Winter comes at last,
> And shuts the scene."

But why should Autumn make us melancholy? If we have improved the bounteous smiles of Heaven, every day may and *will* have its share of joy.

Yet neither the picturesqueness of the Palisades, nor the grander beauty of the highlands, nor the elegant villas of the merchant princes of Gotham, built on the bluffs, interested him then, for his mind was continually reverting to the idol of his heart, and he was too unhappy to derive pleasure from surrounding objects. After pacing to and fro on the hurricane deck for some time, Eugene descended to the cabins to take a look at his fellow passengers, and found they numbered over three hundred, all on various errands bent; and they certainly presented a motley assembly. Almost every State in the Union was represented, and there were also many foreigners.

At one end of the cabin stood a band of politicians, discussing the affairs of the nation with as much anxiety as if each had the care of government upon his own shoulders; and at the other, a group of emigrants were talking about their prospects in the "far West." In the ladies saloon, old and young ladies, children and nurses were amusing themselves in different ways; some employed with their needlework, others walking about, many reclining on the elegant softly cushioned sofas and divans, and several employed in reading either magazines, or the last new novel.

Here Buckingham remained some time, contrasting the beauty of some of the really charming young girls with that of his Julia; and in his eye, none could compete with her.

The day sped onward—and towards evening the boat arrived at Albany, where Eugene concluded to stop until the next night. In the morning he went abroad to view the city and its environs, and after dinner retired to his room to sleep for a few hours, as he was to travel in the night train for Buffalo. Six o'clock found him in the cars rapidly skimming through green fields, valleys, rocks, and over little streams and great rivers also. Darkness came and still the train sped on, occasionally stopping, at which times our traveller with other passengers would step out to look around him. The night was clear and the stars gleamed—and when he would return to his seat and endeavor to slumber, he found it impossible. The next day he felt so tired and sleepy that he scarcely looked about him, and was rejoiced when the train stopped at Buffalo. Here he remained all night, and in the morning started in the train for Niagara. Towards the middle of the day the *hoarse roaring* of the mighty cataract sounded upon his ear. His feelings were then changed from melancholy gloom to awe and reverence; and when the cars stopped, he left his baggage to be taken to the Cataract House, and without delay bent his steps towards Iris Island, where, as he stood, the falls beneath him

"Exerting all his soul,
"To take the vast idea in, and comprehend the whole;"

he could not help exclaiming—

"These are thy works, Parent of good!
"Almighty! Thine this universal frame:
"Thyself how wondrous then!"

That evening he penned the following for the Fall's Register:

"White-foaming, boiling river,
Thy rapids ceaseless roar,
For ever, on for ever,
Till Time shall be no more.

"I hear thee, now I hear thee—
At evening's silent hour;
Whenever I am near thee
I feel thy magic power.

"Green be the waters ever
Wreathed with a foam of snow,
Flow on, majestic river,
Unstemm'd, resistless, flow!"

At Niagara our hero remained two days, viewing the Falls at every accessible point. On the eve of his departure for Chicago he retired to his room and wrote to his ever present idol, thus:

"DEAR LADY,

"Amid the glorious beauty and grand sublimity of Niagara, *I feel alone.* Amid the gay and fashionable throng of visiters here, my mind reverts incessantly to you. Oh! that we could become nearer related! that I could call you by a nearer and dearer name! But, alas! I fear that I am destined to be a wanderer, banished from the endearments of love. However, wherever I am, my *heart* is always with you. Your image is constantly before me. I often recal to mind the happy hours I have spent in your sweet society—the delightful ramble we took together in Greenwood some time ago, admiring the flowers—my mind being occupied the while by a *fairer flower*. Oh, that I could obtain *that flower* to adorn my Southern parterre! You cannot imagine, dearest, with what intensity I love you—with what utter loneliness my heart is filled when I am away from you.

"Think of me sometimes in your nightly orisons, and pray for your unhappy

"EUGENE."

Our traveller left Buffalo by the Oregon, and here again encountered a severe storm. He had not been long on board before

"The waters darkened, and the rustling sound
"Told of the coming gale."

Black clouds were driven on in thick array, and big drops of rain along with strong gusts of wind soon ripened into a storm, whose fury became every moment greater. The passengers were much terrified, and at one time the Captain almost despaired of saving the vessel. But, after some hours the tempest gradually abated, and the sun struggling through the dense clouds, shone brightly and clear over that vast inland sea, Lake Erie.

At length the Oregon arrived at Detroit, at which event, Eugene, as well as many of his fellow passengers, rejoiced, for they had suffered much from the Lake sickness during their trip.

At this city he remained a short time, and then started for Chicago, which he reached in a couple of days. He was so much pleased with the beauty of this place that he spent several days in its vicinity. He frequently ascended the cupola of the Lake House, and with the aid of a telescope viewed a vast and boundless prairie on one side, and on the other could see for miles over the dark green waters of lake Michigan. As it was, he enjoyed in a measure the beautiful scenery around him, but would have appreciated it far better had the melancholy which continually preyed upon his mind been removed. Owing to this Eugene became quite unwell, and when he left Chicago, in the stage for Peru, he was not fit to be out of bed, as he was in a high fever. For two nights he got no sleep, and on the second was rendered much worse by being terrified at the sight of a burning prairie, through which their journey lay.

The night was clear, and a slight breeze agitated the air. As the stage, drawn by four spirited horses, advanced rapidly through the prairie, a sense of smoke began to be perceived by the passengers, and looking out they saw, apparently several miles in advance of them, a great volume of smoke illuminated by a brilliant, spreading flame, which appeared to be many miles in extent. As they drew gradually nearer, all, including our invalid traveller, acknowledged that although a fearful, it was a splendid sight. The beaten track alone remained untouched, which, as far as the eye could see, seemed like a black serpent meandering through the prairie; while on both sides of it vast sheets of flame waved and pointed in the air through the thick black smoke, like so many demons exulting in their terrible career of destruction.

Still the stage advanced, for it could not go back, and the bright flame came sweeping onward to meet it with frightful vehemence. The driver now urged his frightened horses to a full gallop, fearing, as did the passengers, that the flames might attach themselves to the vehicle as it was, the heat and smoke nearly blinded and almost suffocated them. But onward they went, scathless, for a full mile, and the blaze began to decrease—at last to be extinguished, leaving after it nothing but a black desolation. At length the weary and trembling steeds were suffered to relapse into a trot; and when the escaped travellers looked behind them, they saw in the distance the same bright, awful ocean of flame careering onward with the same devouring fury.

All were terrified in a more or less degree, but Eugene, from his illness, felt the effects of his fright much more than the others, and has often said, that to the last day of his life he would never forget that night of terror.

The following soul-stirring lyric, descriptive of a burning prairie, will be read with interest wherever a taste for American scenes and incidents prevails:

THE PRAIRIE ON FIRE!

BY GEORGE P. MORRIS.

The following ballad is founded, in part, upon a thrilling story of the West, related by Mr. Cooper, the novelist.

The shades of evening closed around
The boundless prairies of the West,
As, grouped in sadness on the ground,
A band of pilgrims leaned to rest:
Upon the tangled weeds were laid,
The mother and her youngest born,
Who slept, while others watch'd and pray'd,
And thus the weary night went on.

Thick darkness shrouded earth and sky—
When, on the morning winds there came
The Teton's shrill and thrilling cry,
And heaven was pierced with shafts of flame;
The sun seem'd rising through the haze,
But with an aspect dread and dire!
The very air appeared to blaze!
O God! the prairie was on fire!

Around the centre of the plain
A belt of flame retreat denied,
And, like a furnace glowed the train
That wall'd them in on every side:

And onward rolled the torrent wild—
  Wreaths of dense smoke obscured the sky!
Down knelt the mother and her child,
  And all—save one—shrieked out " We die!"

" Not so!" he cried—" help—clear the sedge!
  " Strip bare a circle to the land!"
That done, he hastened to its edge,
  And grasped a rifle in his hand:
Dried weeds he held beside the pan,
  Which kindled at a flash, the mass!
Now " fire fight fire!" he said, as ran
  The forked flames among the grass.

On three sides soon the torrent flew,
  But on the fourth no more it raved!
Then large and broad the circle grew,
  And thus the pilgrim band was saved!
The flames receded far and wide,
  The mother had not prayed in vain!
God had the Teton's arts defied!
  His scythe of fire had swept the plain.

But, to proceed with our story: on reaching Pern our traveller took a boat to St. Louis, and from that place another to Nashville, making as little delay as possible on account of his illness. Before he reached the last mentioned place, while walking one morning on the hurricane deck, he suddenly fell down in a swoon. One of his fellow passengers, who happened at heart to be a "good Samaritan," came to his assistance, raised him in his arms, and with the help of one or two others carried him to his berth, where this true friend attended him and procured him medicine until he seemed to grow better; while many of the other passengers, like the "Priest and the Levite," passed by without deigning to notice him.

How soothing to the sick in a strange land, the welcome attentions of a stranger! 'Tis like a dream of home. Eugene felt this, and was deeply grateful.

After arriving at Nashville he took passage in the stage for Huntsville, Alabama, which started some time before day. There was but one passenger besides himself, and the journey would be a long one.

And now, sad to relate, since Eugene had left Chicago he had suffered so much both bodily and mentally, that his illness terminated in brain fever, and he became suddenly, helplessly *insane.*

But, I will give the account of his derangement in his own words, as related to me after his restoration; for, unlike many of the insane, he perfectly remembered every circumstance that occurred during his unfortunate malady.

CHAPTER VIII.

"See how the noble mind's o'erthrown."

"I know not how the case may be,
"I tell the tale as told to me."

"I left Nashville about five o'clock in the morning, for Huntsville, and in the stage was but one passenger beside myself. He was a perfect stranger to me, a gentleman from Kentucky, who was going on by Charleston to one of the eastern cities, in order to embark for Europe. His name was Stanley, his age about thirty, and he possessed a kind and benevolent physiognomy, which accorded well with his actions towards me during my unfortunate malady. I have always looked upon this crisis in my illness as a remarkable special Providence—a blessing from heaven, that this man should have been placed in my way to protect me on my journey home.

"The morning was rather cool, and I had my buffalo robe wrapped about me; but though I was chilled in body, there was a burning fever in my brain. I had never in my life before felt as I did then, yet for a time I conversed calmly and rationally with my fellow passenger. But, when we had got about thirty miles from Nashville, suddenly I experienced a feeling exactly similar to an electric shock vibrating through every fibre of my frame, and from that moment I was insane.

"I started up, and throwing off my cap, pulled the buffalo over my head, and began shouting loudly; gesticulated with my arms, and threw myself into all sorts of attitudes. This paroxysm lasted for several minutes, and then subsided slowly. I think I shall never forget the looks of Stanley as he appeared when I became calm enough to observe him. He was crouched into the farthest corner of the stage, his face of an ashy paleness, and his eyes glaring wildly with affright. When I spoke to him he scarcely answered, and seemed to expect every moment would be his last.

"My intellect was still clouded, and I told him solemnly not to mention the miracle he had just seen performed on me—for I was now a spiritual being. Indeed, my first impression was, that my guardian angel had stood on one side of me and the evil spirit on the other, and that there had been a terrible strife between them as to which should gain possession of me; but as the former became victorious, I was endowed, in some mysterious way, with the powers of a celestial being, and would soon mount to Heaven, like some of the prophets of olden time.

"However, at intervals I conversed quite rationally with my fellow passenger, whose fears had in some degree subsided; but on reaching Columbia I was attacked with another paroxism, and leaping out of the stage as it stopped, I commenced shouting and running about the streets, attracting the attention of a great number of people.

"There is a high bridge crossing the Duck river at this place: it is built upon the perpendicular rocks of this rapid stream; and to this bridge I sprang with the intention of leaping from it into the river, imagining that, as I was *immortal*, there was no danger of being drowned. But as I was in the act of making the fatal plunge, my friend Stanley fortunately reaching the spot in time, seized me, and, assisted by some of the bystanders, carried me off, not without some trouble, to the hotel, where I remained a short time, amusing the persons around me by my actions and conversation, which were wild in the extreme.

"At length, when the stage stopped at the door for us they attempted to get me into it, but in vain; I was determined not to leave the hotel. They caused it to drive away a short distance in hopes that I would change my mind, but in this they were mistaken, and Stanley was obliged to let our baggage go on without us.

"Towards evening this paroxysm abated, and I ordered my friend to procure me a bath, which he cheerfully attended to, as he knew it was best to comply with my requests if at all reasonable. We were then conducted into a back room, in which there blazed a cheerful fire, but even here I was not secure from impertinent curiosity, for many persons followed us to this retreat. It was very wrong, and I thought so at the time, to allow them admittance.

"When Stanley took off part of my clothing, preparatory to putting me in the bath, he found a money-belt buckled around my waist. This gave rise to many conjectures, concerning myself and my profession. Some of the bystanders thought me a merchant going to the Eastern cities for goods; others, that I was a drover; but most of them imagined, more correctly, that I was merely travelling for amusement. At length one person seeing my name marked on part of my clothing, inquired, with a great deal of interest, if I was not the son of Col.

Buckingham, of Charleston. This man, no doubt, was acquainted with my father, but being very jealous of my dignity, I would not deign to answer him.

"At last I ordered the room to be cleared, which was no sooner done than I made a rush to the door, stripped as I was, to my under garments, in order, as I said, to make my ascension into the upper regions. However, I was soon brought back by my friend Stanley, and in a short time after bathing I was put to bed. I became calmer after a while, and slept some during the night.

"The next day being Sunday, I objected to start in the stage for Pulaski, as I considered it very wrong to travel on that holy day, but by much persuasion my kind friend got me in the vehicle. The passengers besides Stanley and myself were two ladies and a gentleman. Before we had proceeded far I again became excited and commenced talking about my aerial ascension, which alarmed the females very much. However, I was not violent just then, and when I ceased talking, I saw they regarded me with a great deal of sympathy, particularly, as during my ravings I had repeatedly called upon *my darling Julia.* They conversed with Stanley concerning me, and their conjectures were, alas! too true: that I had been disappointed in love, which was the cause of my present deplorable condition. Oh, ye unreasonable and hard hearted parents! what will ye not have to answer for, by thus causing, or being the means of, the greatest affliction that can visit poor human nature.

" As we proceeded on our journey I became very rude and troublesome, so much so that my companions were obliged to place my buffalo robe between them and me to protect themselves from my ill conduct. As is generally the case with insane persons, strange as it may seem, I treated my *best* friend worse than any other person, for I spat in poor Stanley's face, struck him, and called him all manner of hard names whenever he attempted to render me any service.

" When the stage stopped to change horses, or to give the passengers an opportunity for refreshments, I was generally shut up in the vehicle by myself, which always rendered me very indignant, and I would rave and shout so loud as to draw a crowd around me. Then I would begin to complain of Stanley's wicked behavior, telling those around me that he was Satan himself, to find whom I had travelled all over the world, and having caught him, was now taking him to shut him up in the infernal regions, where he properly belonged. One reason why my insane ideas ran so much on this point, was, because I had visited, a short time previous to my illness, a representation, at one of the Western museums, of the place of punishment, which we call Hell. I will give a concise description of it as it exists in my memory.

"The room in which it is exhibited is at first quite dark, and an unearthly sound, something like distant thunder, strikes upon the ear. In a few moments the place becomes a little lighter, and the curtain rising, the spectator beholds a frightful sight. Near the front of the stage appears in 'bold relief,' Belzebub himself, the commander in chief of those doleful regions.

> 'Black he stands as night, and shakes a dreadful dart;'

While near him stands the great dog Cerberus, with three heads, who guards the gates of Hell. This infernal monster keeps up an awful howling, and springs forward occasionally, as if he intended to devour some of the spectators. On the other side of Satan is an enormous black snake, who is continually coiling and uncoiling his long body in the attempt to reach some hapless mortal, his huge jaws wide open, and his forked tongue trembling therein. Some of the spectators who happen to stand near, start back with fearful apprehension.

"The room is represented with great rocks hanging over it, some of their points nearly touching the floor. At the farther end is a large fire whereon *skeletons are roasting.* Chains are rattling—demons are howling—mournful cries are resounding through the dismal regions, and the lost spirits are heard calling to one another, inquiring the cause of each other being sent thither. Every one tells a tale of sin, while curses and revilings echo on all sides—and at the same time that *unceasing, doleful thundering sound* is heard,

> 'A universal hubbub wild
> 'Of stunning sounds and voices all confused,
> 'Borne through the hollow dark;'

while at the same time the olfactories are saluted with a strong sense of brimstone.

"I never was so glad to escape from any place in my life as I was from this horrid spectacle, and a cold chill runs through my frame yet, when I think of it. I consider it highly improper for authorities of cities to permit such exhibitions in their precincts, as there are many nervous persons who may be affected by the sight for months and years afterwards.

"To proceed: on arriving at Pulaski I jumped out of the stage and began running about the streets and shouting as I had done at Columbia. I had not proceeded far when I was surrounded by half a dozen men, who, thinking there was danger in leaving me at liberty, secured me, but not before I had knocked down a couple of them. They then bound me with cords and carried me off to jail. On the way I complained of being hurt by the tightness of my bonds, and my captors were lenient enough to stop and loosen them. I kept continually asking these men what I had done to be used thus harshly, but disregarding my inquiries, they hastened to put me in a room of the prison. At this juncture my true friend came to my aid, and after much expostulation I was allowed to be taken to a hotel, where I was bled and put to bed. As Stanley was nearly worn out from attending me, another person was put into my room to take charge of me, but he proved a bad nurse and I suffered very much on account of his inattention. My arm was bandaged so tightly that it threw me into a fever and I became very thirsty, but could not prevail on my attendant either to give me a drink or to loosen my bandage; and thus I remained suffering until the doctor came the next morning."

CHAPTER IX.

"The lunatic, the lover and the poet,
"Are of imagination all compact."—*Shakspeare.*

"Many persons labor under a mistake in regard to the insane, they imagine that they have no physical suffering, whereas, their sensibilities are much more acute than those of the sane. Owing to the raging fever within me, I suffered more from thirst than from anything else during my journey, yet could not make my attendants believe that I wanted to drink almost constantly.

"In the morning Stanley hired a private carriage to take us to Huntsville, Alabama, as I was too troublesome to the stage passengers. After reaching this place, I was brought on to Whitesville, on the Tennessee River, and there put on board a steamboat bound for Chattanooga, Tennessee. On arriving at this town, they placed me in the cars for Charleston, where we arrived after night. I was taken by the faithful Stanley to my father's house, in a carriage, and the family aroused from their slumbers. You may imagine the grief and consternation of my father and sister when they beheld the unfortunate Eugene brought home to them, a wreck both in body and mind. They were nearly distracted, and the slaves went about weeping for 'poor massa Eugene,' for I had been a general favorite among them, as they were always treated by me with kindness and humanity.

"When my friend Stanley hinted to my father his suspicions in regard to the cause of my insanity, the old man's heart smote him, and he bitterly repented what he had done; but repentance, as it often does, came too late, and he felt it deeply.

"When it became known in Charleston that I had been brought home insane, it created a great deal of excitement among my acquaintances. Various were the conjectures as to the cause of my derangement; some thought it was brought on through the excitement of travelling; and others that it was caused by illness; but few knew the true reason; and these few became acquainted with it by being admitted to my presence to assist in taking care of me, at which times they would hear me talking in my delirium of my dear Julia, thus: 'She is dressed in pure white like an angel, and has such a bright, sunny countenance that none can look at her without being dazzled, therefore you must all put on glasses if you would see her.'

"At other times, when I wanted to escape, that I might go to Julia, I would exclaim, 'there is no use in trying to confine me—if I were to exert my strength I would be more powerful than even Samson. If this little world of yours was a ball of solid iron, and I was placed in the centre of it, I would burst it into ten thousand fragments to fly to my Julia; or if this ball of iron was wrought into a great chain, and I fettered with it, I would break it asunder as easily as Samson broke the cords that bound him when told that the Philistines were upon. Such is my strength; but if Julia wished, she could bind me with a single hair of her head; for *love* is the secret of her power.'

"The only way my attendants could force me to eat, or to take any kind of refreshment, was by bringing it to me in a *white* vessel, and telling me it was prepared and sent by Julia; white being my favorite color, because in my imagination she was always dressed in it. If they unthinkingly told me that it was not sent by her, I would dash it on the floor or in their faces.

"Many of my dearest friends and relatives visited me during the time I remained at home, most of whom were affected to tears when they beheld me in this deplorable condition. Great sympathy was manifested towards me by my acquaintances, and prayer was offered for my restoration in some of the churches.

"My true friend Stanley, (the good Samaritan,) Heaven's blessings be ever upon him! was obliged to start immediately for New-York, as the steamer was to leave for England in a few days. On taking his departure, the day after my arrival at home, my father pressed upon him, and obliged him to take, against his inclination, a heavy purse of gold. Although constrained to accept it as well as several presents from my friends, he contended that he had done nothing more than his duty in protecting and assisting a fellow being when in sickness and distress.

"Several physicians were brought in to see me, and all agreed in advising my friends to take me to the Insane Asylum at Columbia, South Carolina, which, under their directions, was attended to.

"I arrived at the Asylum in the night, very weak, and so much exhausted that it was with difficulty I could walk or even stand, as I had slept and ate very little since I was first attacked. Soon after my arrival, Dr. Thomson, physician of the establishment, came to examine my case, and made several inquiries of my friends concerning me. After giving me some medicine, I was locked up in a room for the night.

"The next morning I was let out in the hall among the other patients, and immediately began to imagine myself in the mansion of Dr. Tennyson, at New-York. I thought the persons around me were his servants, and ordered them about as such. I demanded of them why the doctor and Julia did not make their appearance, as I had sent up my card. *En passant*, I would remark that I verily believe, had Julia really presented herself before me at this juncture, it would have been the means of my immediate restoration. However, the officers of the Institution encouraged these fancies, talking of the Doctor and enlarging upon the beauty and accomplishments of the lady, until I grew very much pleased with them, and became quite docile.

"As I frequently heard music in some of the rooms, I concluded it was Julia's piano, and wondered why she used me so cruelly; not deigning to make her appearance.

"Thus passed several days. At length I began to improve both in body and mind, and was taken out daily by an attendant to promenade in the beautiful garden attached to the Asylum. I was always fond of flowers, and while there their presence had a great influence upon me. It was early spring; and the first timid blossoms were opening to the sun. While wandering around the alleys and flower beds of this favorite resort, a gentle yet sweet melancholy would pervade my whole being, and I would experience a strange sort of happiness that seemed almost unearthly.

"The greatest trouble my attendants had with me was to make me take my medicine, which was always excessively nauseous. If I could, I would always dash the vessel containing it to the floor, breaking it in a thousand pieces. I shall never forget one time when I threw the bowl containing some bitter ingredient into the face of one of the assistants. Immediately three strong rough men seized me, and throwing me on the floor, forced open my teeth, and poured the medicine down my throat so fast as nearly to strangle me. This was the hardest treatment I received while there; and I have always thought that the kind superintendent was not aware of this circumstance, as my brutal attendants would have been severely rebuked.

"There is great room for improvement in regard to the character and qualifications of attendants in insane asylums, for in managing a maniac, talents of the same kind are required as in the moral training and education of children, or, as evinced by the kind and sympathysing physician: but, instead of possessing these qualifications, those men are often rough, uneducated, unfeeling wretches, who are not fit to take care of a horse, much less a human being whose mind is diseased, and who consequently requires the most gentle and considerate treatment.

"But to return to my own case. After getting a good deal better, the Doctor told me where I was, and the reason of my being brought there. This was the first time I had been told that I was insane, which I think should have been made known to me long before, for such persons are generally the last to believe themselves deranged.

"After being made aware of my infirmity, I took my medicine and baths without much trouble, although the latter were pretty hard to bear, being nearly scalding, while at the same time very cold water was poured upon my head.

"As I became more improved, I was sent out in a carriage with other patients, accompanied by an attendant, to see the public buildings and grounds about Columbia, such as the State House, the College, the cotton factories on the Congarie River, &c. I was soon taken to better apartments, where I had the liberty of occupying a handsome parlor, containing a piano and other musical instruments, together with a number of books and papers for the use of the patients. I also went to the public table, as heretofore my allowance had always been sent to me. I often attended concerts, and lectures on astronomy and other sciences, given by distinguished professors, in that portion of the building set apart for that purpose. The concerts were attended by the improved of both sexes, and they seemed to enjoy them extremely. I think these amusements were very beneficial to the patients.

"About six weeks after I had been admitted to the Asylum, I was pronounced perfectly cured, and consequently discharged by the kind Dr. Thomson, who was admirably suited to his profession as superintendant, by his urbanity, kindness of disposition, and benevolence of heart.

"You may ask whether I suffered much pain, or what was the state of my feelings during my derangement: I can unhesitatingly reply, that with the exception of the rough treatment I received from the ignorant and unfeeling attendants, the few weeks that my reason was dethroned, were to me the happiest of my existence, as I was in extacies most of the time, living in a world of my own creation, a world more bright and beautiful than Arcadian bowers or Elysian fields, having for bosom companions *bright fancies* and *wild imaginations*."

CHAPTER X.

"Ring, joyous chords, ring out again!
"A swifter still and a wilder strain!
"They are here, the fair face and the careless heart,
"And stars shall wane o'er the mirthful part."—*Hemans.*

Being apprised by Dr. Thomson of his son's recovery, Col. Buckingham immediately started for Columbia to bring him home. Their meeting was an affecting one, for the grief his father had felt for the unhappy derangement of Eugene was now turned to joy at having him again restored to the bosom of his family.

They left Columbia in the morning, by railroad, and arrived that evening at Charleston. When they reached Buckingham Hall, they found the slaves, young and old, assembled to welcome their "dear young massa" home. Eugene's heart was so full that tears sprung into his eyes as he beheld their honest joyous faces turned towards him. He shook hands with them all around, while they shouted in unison "God bless young massa Eugene!" The young man was soon obliged to make his escape into the house, for his feelings overcame him. His heart too longed to meet his sister; and as he entered the hall she sprang towards him and fell weeping upon his neck. For several moments neither spoke; and at length Cora exclaimed, "Dear Eugene, how well you look! Thank God! you are home again. But, come in to the dining room, supper is waiting. Come dear father." And they followed her. That evening, to our hero, would have been the happiest of his life, had he then been blest with the presence of his fondly loved Julia; but her name was not mentioned in their conversation; and when all had retired to rest Eugene lay long awake thinking of her, and mentally praying that the great presentiment of his life might one day be accomplished.

The next morning Col. Buckingham, in the fulness of his heart, ordered that there should be a holiday given to the slaves, that they might have a general rejoicing on account of Eugene's happy recovery and restoration to his paternal abode.

"For," said he to his principal overseer, Jerry, in whom he placed great confidence, "Eugene is, in some respects, like the Prodigal Son mentioned in Scripture, 'He was dead and is alive again, he was

p. 113.

THE FESTIVAL.

lost and is found.' So, 'bring hither the fatted calf and kill it, and let us eat and be merry.' "

"Yes, sah!" cried Jerry, with a grin of delight, "all dat an' more sal be done dy—recily."

So away went Jerry to communicate the news of a holiday and festival in honor of their beloved "massa Eugene's" return.

Shortly, loud shouts of merriment echoed through the little hamlet of the slaves, and as the hours passed away all were dressed in their gayest and their best, dancing, singing and chattering in every part of the shady lawn.

Col. Buckingham, with his son and daughter, came forth to see the amusements of the slaves; and the better to view them, they ascended a staircase around a large sycamore tree, which staircase terminated in a platform large enough to contain a dozen persons. While they remained seated here, overshadowed by the large thick leaves above and around them, the colored folks below kept up their glee without cessation.

There were several of the slaves who were tolerable musicians, and these having formed a band, played occasionally in the summer evenings in the lawn before the hall, for the amusement of the family. These were now ranged apart from the rest, near a sparkling fountain between the sycamore and the mansion, and even to the refined ears of the Colonel and his children, "discoursed most elegant music." The leader of the band was Jerry, who sat on top of a hogshead with his legs hanging over the side, doing great execution with his "fiddle and his bow." The others performed on banjoes, bones and other instruments, and were seated around their leader, some on the ground and some on rude benches brought from the cabins.

The residue of the slaves were either lolling on the grass, or sitting beneath the trees, or leaning against the trunks of them, or dancing merrily on the soft, green turf; while others were partaking of the "fatted calf" and drinking something that they thought better than water.

So the day passed in merriment and pleasure, and as the sun began to hide himself behind the clustering trees, the slaves gradually ceased their amusements and commenced clearing the "camp furniture" from the scene of action. Before dark all were again gathered into their cabins, and the Colonel and his family having returned to the Hall, peace and quietness reigned over the scene.

The next day Col. Buckingham, while conversing with his son, introduced the subject of his passion for Julia. "Eugene," said he, "do you still entertain for Miss Tennyson the regard you once had?"

The young man seemed startled, and his countenance glowed as he replied, "I shall love her always, sir."

"My son," then resumed his father, "I feel that I have been to blame in endeavoring to force your inclinations—I feel that I have been partly the cause of your misfortune, and I would fain atone for it. I will not refuse my consent any longer, if you wish to marry her."

Eugene's delight sprang to his eyes and irradiated his whole countenance. He took his father's hand and raised it to his lips. "Thanks, dear father. I have only to gain the consent of Dr. Tennyson."

"What! has he withheld his consent?" exclaimed the Colonel, somewhat surprised. "I thought I was the only bar to your union."

"No sir: Dr. Tennyson, unfortunately, is as much prejudiced against the South and its institutions, as you have been against the North. To convince you of this I will show you his letters to me on the subject."

There was a pause of a few minutes, when Eugene suddenly exclaimed, "Miserable, that I am! what avails your consent, my father? Think you

Julia would wed a man who has been the inmate of a *madhouse?*" And the bright look faded from his countenance, and a shade of despair occupied its place.

"Hush! my son; these are strong words. Calm yourself. If Julia is a sensible woman and really *loves* you, your derangement will have no weight with her. She will consider that it was a dispensation of Providence, and will feel that your sufferings have endeared you to her all the more. Write to her; for she knows all that has befallen you from her cousin, to whom Cora and myself have several times written; write to her, and you will find my words to be correct."

Eugene took his father's advice, and that very evening wrote a long letter to Miss Tennyson, detailing his unfortunate derangement, and concluded thus:

"If you think that this misfortune is a sufficient cause for breaking the engagement we entered into before I left you, you are at liberty to act your pleasure in regard to it. Although my regard for you is deeper than words can express, I would not wish to make your future life unhappy with regrets at marrying a man who had been the inmate of a lunatic asylum. Pardon me if I speak too plainly——

"But, if you have the same affection for me that

you once had, and your father does not oppose you, will you accept one who cannot be happy without you? If I have been insane, it has been altogether on your account—and I entreat you to consider this before you decide."

Julia was much affected when she read his letter, and immediately laid it before her father. He appeared at the time to take little notice of it; but, as weeks flew by, and his daughter's lovely cheek grew paler and paler, like

"The last rose of summer, left drooping alone,"

he could not avoid seeing that her health was rapidly declining, and at last he relented. Calling her to him one day he told her, as she stood before him trembling with apprehension of some stern mandate, that if she was so much attached to Eugene, as not to be happy without him, he would withdraw his former prohibition, and that the nuptials should be solemnized whenever the lovers thought proper.

Joyfully and gladly did Julia hasten to write to the man of her heart, assuring him of her father's consent, and telling him that she never harbored such a selfish idea as that of breaking her engagement on account of his unfortunate aberration of mind.

At the same time Eugene received Julia's letter, his sister got one from Melville, in which he entreated of her, now that her brother was again with his family, that she would no longer delay the day of their union. After consulting with her father and Eugene, she replied to her lover, appointing a day in the month of April, which by this time was not far distant. She also requested of Arlington, at her brother's wish, to persuade the Doctor to accompany him South with his daughter, for nothing would delight her more than to have Julia for her bridesmaid. Eugene, too, wrote again to his beloved, requesting the same favor, and beseeching her to name an early day for their nuptials. In a short time two answers were received, with the tidings that they would all soon be on their way South, Julia telling her lover that she would not appoint their marriage day until after Cora's wedding. With this he was obliged to remain content.

Eugene now thought himself the happiest mortal upon earth. His long treasured wish, his *great presentiment* was about to be realized. He was soon to be possessed of a beautiful, talented, and accomplished woman, a model for her sex, and the sole empress of his affections, upon whose throne was placed the thoughts and aspirations of years.

Cora too had lost some of her former indolence,

and was vastly improved in consequence. She was engaged with her dress-makers and milliners, preparing her *trousseau* for the bridal day. The Colonel himself was happy in the happiness of his children, and now there seemed nothing wanting to constitute earthly felicity.

Before proceeding any further on this subject, we have to inform the reader that Miss Susanna Jones, after the rebuff she had met with from Eugene, never visited the Hall, although her father and the elder Buckingham still remained friends. Cora called on her two or three times, at the request of her father, but there was only cold civility exchanged between them. Susanna still rode, raced and hunted with the young men who visited her father's mansion, but never could get any farther than a flirtation with any of them. She was destined to remain in a state of single blessedness, for her unladylike and disagreeable qualities rendering her unloved, unrespected, and unapproached.

The contention between the Northern and Southern families, like the strife between the Montagues and Capulets, was now at an end. Their misunderstandings were all brought to a close, without any of the melancholy events attending the loves of Romeo and Juliet; and the arrival of the expected guests was daily looked for by the anxious hearts in Buckingham Hall.

At last they came. The meeting of lovers is well understood—I need not describe it. Col. Buckingham received his visitors with the most gentlemanly politeness, and was as much pleased with the Doctor as he was charmed with his lovely daughter.

That evening the young people strolled out through the garden and shady lawn, leaving the elderly gentlemen to discuss their wine, and smoke their segars on the veranda.

The four remained together for a short time, but after a while, as the round moon rose from the tops of the forest trees, and silvered the dew-moistened landscape, Eugene passed with his mistress before a glancing fountain, while the others strolled slowly on. And then the young man, with his sweet Julia leaning upon his arm, lingered to breathe into her ear the heart-felt happiness of his being.

"I could not have lived had you refused me, dearest: yet after my unfortunate derangement I feared ——"

"Eugene! Did you really believe for a moment that your illness would have any weight with me? I look upon what you have undergone as I would upon any other disease. We are not to murmur at the dispensations of Providence. No, Eugene; I feel that I love you better now, for I know that you have suffered for *me.*"

As she spoke she raised her soft, bright eyes to his, with a look of the most trusting affection. He took her delicate hand and raised it to his lips.

"Bless you, my own! Dear Julia, forgive me that I have doubted you."

There was a silence of some moments, and then Eugene said softly, "Do you remember, Julia, that you promised when we met to name the day of our nuptials?"

"Not till after Cora's wedding, I said," she replied.

"My sister will be married in a few days—why then delay? Why should you keep me in suspense? Let me have an epoch to hang my hopes upon.

"Well, to gratify you," replied the lady slowly, "I will name—let me see—yes, the fifth of May, which is my birth day."

Eugene now folded his arms around her and pressed his *first* kiss upon her unresisting lips. They then wandered on among the fragrant flowers, the scented shrubbery and the tall, shady trees, until they were summoned from their world of romance to the dull realities of the tea table, where Cora and Melville had arrived before them.

CHAPTER XI.

"If to do were as easy as to know what were good to do, chapels had been churches and poor men's cottages, princes' palaces."—
Shakspeare.

After tea the young people gathered around the centre table, while the Colonel and Doctor Tennyson sat apart conversing on different subjects. The evening passed very agreeably to all, especially when the two elderly gentlemen joined in the youthful circle and enlivened it with their pleasant jokes.

Col. Buckingham was charmed with the beauty and accomplishments of our heroine, and did not at all wonder that Eugene should have been so enslaved by her. He asked her to play and sing, which, as the others joined in the request, she immediately rose to do. Eugene sprang to escort her to the piano, when his father pushing him aside, said gaily, "Out of the way, sir! Do you think *I* have no claim to this lady? Do you want to monopolize her entirely?" And gallantly offering his arm, he bore off Julia in triumph. They all laughed, of course, and Julia, being seated at the piano, commenced playing. She was a fine performer, and so gratified her hearers that even the slaves assembled outside on the veranda to hear the music, for the negroes are always delighted with the sounds of harmony.

Julia had sung two or three fashionable songs, when the Colonel begged her to sing something of her own composing, "For," said he, "I am aware that you are a poetess."

A slight blush clouded her cheek, and hesitating a moment, she unaffectedly complied.

SONG.

I cannot prize the heart that burns
  For *ev'ry* form of grace,
I cannot love the eye that turns,
  To *ev'ry* fair young face.
The smile that to the lip doth start,
  For *all*, is dear no more;
O, give me a *devoted heart*,
  That *never* loved before!

When this is found, then I can love
  With fervor, pure, intense;
A love that would unchanging prove,
  All truth—all innocence.
Yet I'll repel young Cupid's dart,
  And banish him my door,
Until I find a faithful heart
  That *never* loved before.

Eugene stood by the side of his betrothed, and whispered softly, "You have found that 'faithful heart' at last, that heart 'that never loved before,' have you not dear Julia?"

She smiled, blushed and whispered something in return which was not heard by the others.

By request of the Colonel Julia played and sung several other original pieces, all of which gave the old gentleman infinite pleasure.

But the slaves who were assembled on the veranda, now and then taking the liberty of peering from behind the window curtains into the parlor, were scarcely more delighted with the music than they were impressed by the beauty and elegance of the Northern lady.

Dr. Tennyson was seated on a lounge near one of the windows, and overheard with much amusement the remarks of the sable auditors.

"Oh!" exclaimed Sam, the coachman, "dat ar song am beautiful, deelightful!"

"She sing like a nighturngale," said Judith, the cook, "me no wonder massa Eugene fall in lub wid her."

"He neber could help it," rejoined Drusilla, the old housekeeper, "caze why, she'd sing right trough his heart. 'Pears like massa Buckingham tink so now—look dah! he sits so close to her an' he look at her all de time. I'se 'feared dat he fall in lub wid her his own seff."

The Doctor now beckoned to Melville, who was sitting near the piano with Cora. As he came, the old gentleman pointed over his shoulder towards the window without speaking. Melville smiled and sat down beside him.

After a pause Drusilla observed, "what dat massa Eugene say about missy Julia long 'go? Some po'try—lem me tink.

> 'De beauty ob her brow might put out de stars,
> 'An' make de candles burn de brighter.'"

"O sho!" exclaimed Sam, "*you* talk po'try, haw! haw! dat make me laugh."

"Why you laugh? What fur, I say? You knows nottin'—you big ig'ramus."

"Knows more dan you, fur all dat."

"You go long! Tell me dis den—why ole massa wanter perwent massa Eugene fur to hab dis hansum missy Julia? Why he do dat, an' be de cause ob his dreffful c'lamity. Kin you 'lucidate dat ar' question?"

"You doesn't know it you seff," replied Sam doggedly.

"Doesn't I!" exclaimed Drusilla. "'Pears like I doesn't. How you 'spects I kin live in dis yere house allers, an' not know de princ'pal 'vents of de fam'ly? Lar sakes! does you tink I's deaf an' blind?"

"Tell us den—we like to know."

"Find out fur yourseff den. I shan't condersend fur to hexpose de secrets ob *dis* fam'ly to nobody."

"Will you hush!" said Judith, "how kin we hear missy Julia play, an' you 's makin' sich a clatter?"

"Sho' nough!" rejoined Drusilla, "if nobody listens, she'll be 'wastin' her sweetness on de darkey's ear.'"

On this, the two gentlemen laughed outright, which caused the slaves to make their exit to the lower regions in double quick time.

This little by play being related by the Doctor to the others, caused a considerable degree of merriment.

In the morning, after breakfast, the Colonel offered to show his guest over the mansion and plantation, which offer being much relished by the Doctor, they proceeded first to the observatory, where the latter was much pleased with a fine view of the surrounding country and the bay of Charleston. After glancing at the Colonel's library, which, as I said before, was fitted up in this place, the Doctor and his friend descended to some of the other apartments, which were used as bed-chambers. They were elegantly finished, and furnished with every comfort and luxury, and appeared to be kept in the most perfect order. They then proceeded to the parlors, and withdrawing-rooms on the first floor. These bore the same evidence of taste and elegance—turkey carpets covered the floors, rich damask curtains shaded the windows, and beautiful velvet covered chairs, sofas and ottomans were tastefully arranged through the rooms. The doors were mahogany, with silver hinges and handles, and marble mantles, supported by graceful statues, were surmounted by the rarest of Italian vases and other ornaments of agate and alabaster. One room, especially, the great parlor, as it was called, was ornamented by richly carved and gilded window frames, walls and ceilings painted in fresco; and the furniture was in keeping with the rest.

The porticos or verandas were spacious and airy, well calculated for promenading or lounging in pleasent weather.

Lastly, the gentlemen descended into the basement, where, without elegance there was neatness and comfort. Everything bore a pleasing and cheerful aspect, even the countenances of the slaves, who were busily employed in divers ways, seemed to indicate perfect contentment. These last, at the entrance of their master and his guest bowed and courtesied respectfully; and two or three little woolly heads creeping up to the Colonel, caught hold of the skirt of his coat, singing out, "Me berry good boy, massa; gim me penny."

"You see," said Buchingham, throwing some coppers among them, "how I spoil these creatures."

"Aye," replied the other, "but all masters are not like you."

"Granted," said the Colonel, as they stepped from the back door into the garden, and proceeded slowly down a gravel walk towards Cora's favorite retreat, the arbor before mentioned, "granted, but I foresee that you will one day admit, in spite of prejudices, that there really are no such barbarians among us as you have always believed there were."

"Perhaps I may, but I do not feel inclined to do so just at present."

After remaining a short time in the arbor, they took their way from the garden into the lawn, visited a sparkling fountain, where gold and silver fish abounded, and then mounted a spiral staircase, around a large sycamore tree, which terminated in a platform eight or ten feet square. This was one of the original ideas of the Colonel, and the Doctor thought it a very novel one.

They proceeded, onward, conversing the while, until they reached the principal gate at the main entrance, where stood the porter's lodges, a couple of small handsome buildings occupied by one of the Colonels overseers and his family. Here they paused awhile, and then went, by a circuitous path, to the rear of the lawn, beyond the flower garden, where stood the cabins of the slaves. As these were pretty much the same as most of the slave-cabins in the South, I need not pause to describe them. There were only a few old women and some small children about them, as the rest were at work in the fields, whither the gentlemen now proceeded.

As they strolled about, looking at the slaves, who were diligently at work, the Colonel pointed out one in particular, who although he took part in the labor seemed to act as an overseer. He was a strong, large man, and apparently the most active among them.

"That," said Buckingham is one of my best men; but when I bought him of my neighbor Harding, whose house you can see through those beech trees yonder, he was the most lazy worthless fellow you can conceive of. His master was always a cruel man—and notwithstanding poor Jerry was severely whipped almost every day, he did not alter in the least.

"Knowing of his ill treatment, and believing that he could be reclaimed by gentle management, I offered to buy him, out of pity. Harding readily agreed to it and I brought him home. Jerry behaved just the same for a while, but I said nothing.

"One day in very hot weather I went out in the field and found him asleep, lying with his face to the sun. I took out my handkerchief and laid it over his ebony features. When he awoke and found what I had done. I was told that he was very much ashamed and mortified, saying, 'Massa was too good to such a wicked nigger.' From this there was a decided improvement in him—and he would work with diligence for a few days, until his old habits of laziness would come on, when he would feign sickness. I would then bathe his head with my own hands, and order two other slaves to sit and fan him. He became so much ashamed at last, knowing that he was so unworthy of such kind treatment, that he suddenly left off all his old tricks, and became one of my trustiest and best workmen. So much for the effects of gentle usage."

While this incident was being related the gentlemen had retraced their steps to the mansion. The young people were sitting in the veranda engaged in lively conversation; and joining them, Buckingham and his guest assisted to pass away the time until dinner.

Towards evening, Eugene and Melville proposed a ride on horseback to the ladies, which was gleefully accepted by them, on condition that the old gentlemen should accompany them. This was not declined, so they started, a gay cavalcade.

On their way they passed the mansion and grounds of Harding. "There," said Buckingham to his friend, "is the residence of Jerry's former master. He is a hard, cruel man, but strange to say, he is a Northerner, from the state of Ohio, and once was a strong abolitionist."

"A planter from the North!" ejaculated the Doctor, "how can that be?"

"The fact is," replied the Colonel, "the plantation was left to him by a relative of his wife, who is from the same state with her husband; but failing to dispose of it to advantage, as he had desired to do, he at last concluded to come and live on it himself in spite of his prejudices. He has been here nine years, and appears to enjoy his capacity of tyrant, for he abuses his slaves worse than any Southerner I ever heard of. Certainly he was not cruel at first, but being naturally despotic, he loved to exercise power where he found it easy to do so, and therefore it grew on him by degrees till he became what he now is

"For some time his brother, who still resides in Ohio, corresponded with and visited him occasionally; but becoming disgusted with him as a slave-holder, broke off all communication with Harding and his family, the Northern brother being an abolitionist.

"This man works his slaves harder than any other planter in the neighborhood, and expects them to do as much in a day as white men; and because they do not he beats and half starves them. His wife, too, is as barbarous as her husband; she is much younger than he, and very gay, goes out a great deal, and often rides on horseback. She owns a beautiful black horse, and is so particular about his keeping, that when he is brought out for her to ride, she always takes a white hankerchief and rubs it over the horse, and if it is the least soiled or dusty, she immediately orders her groom to be whipped.

"Thus, you see that the Northerners make the hardest masters and mistresses. And that is the reason I have never employed a Northerner as an overseer."

"Well, but this case is one in a thousand," rejoined Tennyson, "Northerners never come South to become planters; and this man is, according to your own statement, naturally tyrannical."

"I admit that: but I want to show you how mistaken you are in believing that we Southerners are the only tyrannical masters in the Union."

"From what I have seen so far," replied the Doctor, "I find that good masters *do* exist here. But all are not so."

"I do not pretend to say they are. I could point out to you many who are hard and cruel; but as a general thing, the slaves have reason to be, and are, contented with their condition. But you must see something more of our institutions before I ask you to alter your opinion of us."

As they rode on they came in sight of a fine mansion belonging to a gentleman of the name of Hamilton, and the Colonel observed, "There sir resides a man who represents a large share of our Southerners in his openheartedness and hospitality."

"I have always understood that the Southerners were noted for these qualities," said Tennyson.

"They are so, and justly," replied Buckingham. "This gentleman is hardly ever without guests, and thinks nothing of inviting perfect strangers, and entertaining them for weeks at his house, placing horses and carriages at their disposal. Thus you see there is much truth in the adage that 'warm climates produce warm hearts.'"

In the course of their conversation these gentlemen had lingered behind their companions, but now, as they were called by the young ladies, they hastened to join them, and the equestrians rode on until the shades of evening darkened the landscape, when they returned to Buckingham Hall.

CHAPTER XII.

"To a far land he came, yet round him clung
"The spirit of his own."

The next morning Col. Buckingham ordered the carriage to convey himself and Dr. Tennyson to Charleston, to witness a slave auction that was advertised for that day. They arrived thither a few minutes before ten o'clock, which was the hour specified for the sale, and found many persons sauntering about and making observations on the slaves who were assembled in the slave-market, at the Exchange. This lot had been brought from Virginia.

The hour arrived, and the auctioneer mounting the platform prepared to commence business. The first called to the stand was a boy about nineteen, named Jim. After enumerating his good qualities, the man of the hammer commenced crying him off. The bidding was spirited, as he was a stout, likely boy, and he was soon knocked down to a planter from Georgia for a field hand, at $550.

The next offered was a large muscular middle aged man, who was immediately bid off at $935, for a sugar plantation in Louisiana; and his sister Hannah, a good looking girl, then mounted the stand with a gay air, laughing and talking with the bystanders. She was gaudily dressed, and wore, coquettishly, a scarlet turban on her head. She appeared to relish being sold, as she had a hard master, and expected to be bought by a good one in Charleston. When asked what she could do, she replied that she could "Wash and iron a shirt fit for de President; an' as for doin' up chicken fixin's an' oder kinds ob cookin' an' 'fectionaries, she defied any gal in de Carolinas to beat her." A gentleman of Charleston bought her for $625.

An elderly woman named Maria was then called up. She came forward slowly, and was very critically examined by the spectators. Some asked her if she was sickly, and she replied in the affirmative, when the auctioneer interfered, saying that it was all "D——d nonsense, she was well enough, and only wanted to get clear of being sold for a field hand; but that she was good at housework also." And then he continued, "If she gets lazy give a touch or two with the whip, and I'll engage she'll do your work." He then began some indecent jokes concerning her appearance, observing that whoever bought her, would have an increase of stock before long.

Col. Buckingham, out of pity for her forlorn condition, made a bid for her, and she was knocked down to him for $365.

Dr. Tennyson now intimated that he was weary of this scene, so they left and went to the Jail to see a lot of rice field negroes, placed there for sale. These presented a motley appearance, from the sucking child to the gray haired sire. Most of them were assembled in the jail-yard engaged in different ways. Some of the women were cooking meat and other things, in little pots hung over a fire built on the ground, which as soon as cooked were handed out by the females to the crowd around them, who took them as they were given, with their fingers, and ate with apparent satisfaction.

The Doctor thought it strange their victuals were not cooked and distributed by the keepers, but one of them said that they, the slaves, preferred cooking for themselves.

In another part of the yard, in a building for the purpose, was placed a tread-mill whereon several negroes were engaged grinding out corn for their own consumption. Most of them looked cheerful and contented, but a few seemed sad and dejected enough, as they trod their weary round.

At length the Doctor wished to return, and the

carriage being in waiting, the gentlemen entered it, and arrived at the Hall just at dinner time.

Three or four days passed quickly away. In the mean time the preparations for Cora's wedding were almost completed, and it only wanted a couple of days to the appointed time. The young people were enjoying themselves extremely, rambling about the country and riding and visiting to and from Charleston.

One day there were several ladies and gentlemen from that city spending the day at Buckingham Hall, among whom was a gentleman from New Orleans, who had just come to Charleston from Boston where he had been for some time. He was a jovial, communicative person, and an acute observer of "human events." Buckingham had always held him in high esteem.

These gentlemen, with Dr. Tennyson and some others, sat sipping their wine after dinner, the ladies having retired to the parlor.

The conversation had been turned by a remark of the Doctor's, upon his favorite topic, the slavery question.

"By-the-by," cried Bradford, the gentleman just

introduced, "have you read the new work by Mrs. Stowe, Uncle Tom's Cabin?"

Dr. Tennyson replied in the affirmative, and so also did the Colonel.

"Well Doctor, what do you think of it?" asked Bradford, turning towards him as he laid down his glass.

"I think," replied Tennyson, slowly, "that Mrs. Stowe evinces great knowledge of human nature. Her book is an excellent one; it shows up the cruelty and hard-heartedness of slave-holders in a style worthy of imitation. There is an apparent truthfulness in her whole book that makes it doubly interesting."

"I can't agree with you at all!" broke in Col. Buckingham, "she is a talented woman, I confess, and writes well, but some of her stories are too highly colored and much exaggerated. For instance, the escape of Eliza, the quadroon, would have been very well if we could believe that she leaped *ten feet* across the current in the Ohio river, and scampered over the broken ice like a cat, and all the while with a child in her arms."

"Such a thing *might* have been possible," said Doctor Tennyson. "It seems to me that I have heard of such a circumstance before."

"But, I must say," he continued, "that there is

one thing I don't exactly admire;—little Eva is a sweet, angelic creature, yet she is made by the authoress, the companion of a slave, sitting in his lap and embracing him, as if he were a *brother*. Colonel, did you ever permit *your* daughter such intimacy with your negroes?"

Melville started and looked much concerned at the idea, fixing an uneasy gaze upon Buckingham's face, as he replied, "I certainly did *not*, Doctor, nor do I approve of intimacy such as that."

Arlington drew a sigh of relief, and the Colonel added, "Kindness without familiarity is sufficient to gain the love of these creatures. Mrs. Stowe has exaggerated this somewhat."

"Well," suggested Bradford, "the story of Legree is somewhat unnatural. A writer that wishes to *convince* must not color too highly, or the object aimed at will be overshot."

"You are right, sir," said Buckingham. We Planters well know that no such monsters exist as that Legree. To be sure some of them are cruel in beating their slaves ——"

"My good Colonel," interrupted Dr. Tennyson, "You contradict yourself. Was you not telling me the other day of a barbarous Planter near by, a terrible tyrant, one of whose slaves you bought and reclaimed?"

"My dear Doctor, have you forgotten this man you speak of was a *Northern abolitionist*, and none of our Southern men?"

The old gentleman seemed rather taken down, and remained silent. Buckingham continued, "As I said, although some of our Planters are hard masters, they do not beat their slaves to death, or *burn them alive*, or *murder* them, as Legree is represented to have done."

"Such a man could not have lived in our State," said Bradford, "he would have been lynched in no time."

"I know of no instance where a Planter lives entirely isolated from his neighbors," rejoined the Colonel; I don't see how such a thing is possible, where people are coming and going continually."

"But this man lived in Louisiana," observed Tennyson, "in a part where the country is not very thickly settled."

"I have been in all parts of Louisiana," said Bradford, "and such barbarians as Legree have I never seen; neither do I believe that they exist."

"Gentlemen," said Buckingham, allow your glasses to be filled. Doctor, if you please, answer me one question—are you as much prejudiced against our institutions now as you were before you came here?"

Tennyson hesitated ere he replied, "I allow that

my opinions are somewhat changed. From what I have observed personally, I find they are better than I ever supposed them to be; but sir, do not mistake me," added the Doctor, as he observed a smile of triumph on the countenance of his host, "I am not in favor of slavery—I shall always believe that the system is wrong in principle, and will ever remain opposed to it. But that will not interfere with our personal friendship—we have each a right to our different opinions."

"So be it, then," replied Buckingham. "And now my friend," turning to Bradford, "how did you like your Northern tour?"

"Extremely," replied that gentleman, "but of that another time. I wish to relate a little incident to Dr. Tennyson, of a Yankee abolitionist, which came to my knowledge a short time since: that is, if he has no objection to hear it."

"O, not at all," replied the Doctor, "proceed."

"Mr. Doubleface was a strong abolitionist when at home in the land of steady habits; or, to be more particular, the good city of Boston, where he carried on an extensive mercantile business. I say he was an abolitionist at home, but chameleon like, he could change his colors at pleasure. It so happened, in the course of his mercantile operations, that Mr. Doubleface found it necessary to visit the South, and particularly New Orleans; and when he had proceeded as far as Richmond he came to the conclusion that, as the Scripture says, 'it is not good for man to be alone;' though at the same time he had adopted that maxim years before, for he left a wife and five children in Boston. Recollecting this circumstance, he merely altered the text a little by saying, 'it was not good for man to *travel* alone,' as he needed some one to take care of his linen, &c. and be a companion to him in his lonely hours; therefore, being at a slave sale in Richmond, he concluded to purchase a beautiful quadroon who charmed him greatly by her liveliness, intelligence and wit. The bargain was made; but as he respected appearances, and did not wish so *delicate* an affair to be known, he provided the lady with elegant dresses and jewelry, and called her his wife. Things went on very well for a while, as they proceeded to New Orleans; he, however, contriving to keep the pretty Lucinda as much as possible from the sight of his Southern acquaintances, lest they should discover the secret. Arriving at the Crescent city, he put up at the St. Charles' Hotel, and S. S. Doubleface and lady of Boston, was entered on the register.

"While in New Orleans, this man wrote to his wife in Boston, telling her, among other interesting news, that he had done a great deal of good among the slaves; that he had ameliorated the condition of many, and was daily instilling *moral precepts* into the minds of all with whom he had communication. He said his pity was excited by the bad usage some of them received, and only wished he had the power to prevent the buying and selling of human flesh and blood.

"At the time of writing thus, he was representing to his friends in the South, and particularly those with whom he was transacting business, that he was rather in favor of slavery, and intimated that he might at some future time become a planter himself.

"But a gentleman of his acquaintance, having just arrived in New Orleans from the 'Athens of America,' put up at the same hotel, and was much surprised to see 'S. S. Doubleface and lady' on the register, when he knew he had seen Mrs. Doubleface in Boston the day before he left, and she had told him that her husband was then in New Orleans, having just received a letter from him.

"This gentleman was not long in discovering how matters stood; and disgusted with the vile hypocrisy of Doubleface, threatened to expose him; whereupon the latter suddenly left the city for the North, taking the slave with him.

"They went up the Mississippi and Ohio, as far

as Louisville Kentucky, where, after growing tired of, and abusing his mistress worse than he would a dog, he sold her in that city for half the sum he had given for her. This being the last slave state on his way North, he could not have kept her longer, had he wished."

"I see," said Dr. Tennyson, laughing, "you are all bent upon making a convert of me with your arguments and stories. One thing however I will admit: I shall not go home as strong an abolitionist as I came hither."

Well pleased at this concession, the Colonel arose from the table, saying, "I am glad to hear you say that, my friend."

"And furthermore, I would say that I have carried my prejudices too far in opposing the union of our children," resumed Tennyson, "and have thus been partly the cause of their unhappiness. Colonel, will you not make a like confession?"

"I will—I do, with all my heart," replied Buckingham.

"And now, let us join the ladies,—for I perceive some of our young gentlemen have made their escape while we have been talking."

They all accordingly repaired to the parlor.

CHAPTER XIII.

> "Bring flowers, bring flowers, for the bride to wear,
> "They were born to blush in her shining hair."
>
> "They are gone—they are fled—they are parted all;
> "Alas! the forsaken Hall!"

The morning that was to witness the bridal of Cora and Melville dawned clear and lovely upon them. All preparations had been completed for their departure the next day with Dr. Tennyson and his daughter for New-York, where the nuptials of the latter were to be solemnized.

At ten o'clock, A. M. a numerous assemblage of the *elite* of Charleston, together with many of the Colonel's friends from neighboring States, were awaiting the advent of the bridal train in the great parlor of Buckingham Hall.

At last they entered—the bride looking as interesting as brides always do, arrayed in a splendid white satin, embroidered with silver, and sparkling

p. 146.

with diamonds—a veil of rich lace falling gracefully from her head, fastened by a wreath of orange flowers.

Julia, as bridesmaid, was more simply dressed, in white embroidered silk, pearl bracelets on her arms, and a necklace of the same clasped around her graceful neck. Her hair fell in natural ringlets around her head, which was encircled by a wreath of white rosebuds.

The eyes of all present expressed their undisguised admiration of the beautiful bridesmaid, and many a manly bosom throbbed with envy against Eugene, who alone would possess the brilliant prize.

The reverend gentleman approached, and in a few minutes the ceremony was concluded. The bride and groom then received the congratulations of the company, after which all repaired to the dining-room, where an elegant entertainment graced the "festive board."

In the afternoon, through the kindness and indulgence of Col. Buckingham, the slaves of the plantation were allowed a festival in honor of the wedding. Several gentlemen in the neighborhood, as well as the guests then at the Hall, permitted their slaves to join in the rejoicings.

In the lawn, near the fountain before mentioned, was a long table well spread with substantial eatables and drinkables, whereat were seated a large number of men, women and children, all enjoying themselves to the utmost.

The wedding guests who yet remained at the Hall, together with the bridal party, descended into the lawn to witness the rejoicings. When they reached the fountain the slaves all rose and saluted the bride and groom in their rude fashion, with cheers and acclamations that were almost deafening.

"Holla!" shouted Buckingham, "that will do. Don't frighten the ladies with your roaring."

They were immediately silent; and as the company walked away to another part of the lawn, the negroes commenced tuning up their fiddles and banjoes, while the women cleared away the remnants of the feast, preparatory to the dance on the green sward.

In half an hour's time a couple of hundred men and women, dressed in their best attire, were capering and dancing to the music of the fiddles and banjoes beneath the tall trees of the park, while others were lying about the grass in different places, singing with good musical voices all sorts of lively tunes; some improvising as they went along verses in honor of the bride and groom.

The ladies and gentlemen walked among them much amused at their drollery, both in dancing and singing. Dr. Tennyson, and Julia in particular, who were not accustomed to such scenes, laughed heartily at their strange capers and queer songs.

Buckingham's principal man, Jerry, who was before mentioned, sat surrounded by a circle of boys and girls, who took up the chorus of his impromptu singing, some of which ran thus:

O! missy Cora, she go way,
She got married dis ere day;
When she come back we nebber know,
Mighty sorry dat she go.
Chorus: O, missy Cora, she go way.

Massa Eugene he go too,
Wid de gal he lub so true:
But he soon come back again,
Bring new missy wid him den.
Chorus: O, massa Eugene, he go too.

Massa Melville nice young *coon,*
Gib ole nigger picayune;
Mighty sorry he can't stay,
Case he take young missy 'way.
Chorus: O, massa Melville nice young *coon.*

Good ole Doctor from de Nort',
Treats a nigger as he ort;
Wants to make de darkies free,
Case he tinks dey orter be.
Chorus: O, good ole Doctor from de Nort'.

Darkies dey don't wan' be free,
Case dey happy as dey be:
Massa gibs 'em plenty meat—
Berry apt to fo'git *de treat.*
Chorus: O, darkies dey don't wan' be free.

This song was laughed at and applauded by the auditors; and at length, the shadows beginning to lengthen, the wedding guests returned to the mansion, and shortly after departed for their homes.

Blythe and happy, the slaves retired to their quarters, chattering together about their pleasant holiday; and so closed around them the hours of the evening.

Early the next morning the bridal party were prepared to start. They were to remain in New-York until after Julia's marriage, and then start for a six months' tour in Europe, during which time they were to visit the friends of Melville in England. Col. Buckingham would accompany them as far as New-York to witness his son's nuptials, and then return home. In the meantime the plantation would be left in care of his trusty overseer, and the Hall under the surveillance of the old housekeeper Drusilla, who for years had had the sole control and management of the domestic concerns.

As they were about to depart the slaves crowded around them expressing much sorrow and regret. Rosa, in particular, the favorite young slave of Cora, wept incessantly when she found she could not accompany her mistress, although told that she would undoubtedly be abducted by the abolitionists if she took her to the North, as others had been when taken thither by Southerners. So, although Cora would have liked her attendance, poor little Rosa was obliged to remain in expectation of her mistress' return.

Bidding adieu to the Hall, the little party were driven to Charleston, and embarking on board a steamer, were soon launched on their watery way. They had a short and agreeable passage. When they arrived at the great metropolis, they proceeded at once to Dr. Tennyson's mansion.

The fifth of May at length arrived—and two happy hearts at least, welcomed the eventful day. At nine o'clock, A. M. the wedding guests were assembled in Dr. Tennyson's handsome parlors, awaiting the entrance of the bridal party. It was not long before they made their appearance—and never did Julia look so beautiful. She was attired in white crape covered with lace trimming, plain yet elegant. A gauze veil floated from her head, and a single rosebud decorated her hair. She looked lovely without any ornaments—and as the manly bridegroom gazed on her as she stood by his side, he looked as if he thought

"A seraph not more bright."

Her bridesmaid, a young and pretty girl; and a friend of Eugene's, who stood as groomsman, were the only attendants. They were married by an Episcopal Clergyman; and after the ceremony the dining room was thrown open, where a splendid and *recherche* collation awaited the invited guests.

A couple of hours after, the newly married couples proceeded to the wharf, accompanied by their relatives and friends, who desired to see them start, and embarked in one of Collins' Steamers for Europe. And here we take our leave of them, and also of the reader.

FINIS.

www.ingramcontent.com/pod-product-compliance
Lightning Source LLC
LaVergne TN
LVHW021407110826
845150LV00007B/1819

9781425512446